THE LAW OF RETURN

Short Stories

Maxine Rodburg

Carnegie Mellon University Press
Pittsburgh 1999

THE LAW OF RETURN

Acknowledgments

I hope that all of these people know how important their help and support have been to me: Jo Ann Beard, Suzanne Berne, Kim Cooper, Kathleen Cushman, Jodi Daynard, Sharon Dilworth, Phil Gambone, Alexandra Johnson, Deborah Kaplan, Richard McCann, George Packer, Eileen Pollack, Philip Press, Adam Schwartz, Nancy Sommers, and Jessica Treadway.

The stories in this collection were originally published in the following magazines: "The Law of Return" (as "The Newarker") in *The Georgia Review,* "Days of Awe" in *Belles Lettres,* "March of Dimes" and "The Orphan" in *The Boston Review,* "Pocahontas in Camelot" in *The New England Review,* "Keer Avenue, July 1967" in *The Michigan Quarterly Review,* "The Widower Visarrion" (as "Keer Avenue") in *Agni,* "Concessions" (as "Shelter") in *The Virginia Quarterly Review*

Book Design: Lisa Rump
Cover Design: Becky A. Cowser
Cover Photograph: Maxine Rodburg

Library of Congress Card Catalog Number 98-74658
ISBN 0-88748-313-5 Pbk.
Copyright © 1999 by Maxine Rodburg
Printed and Bound in the United States of America
10 9 8 7 6 5 4 3 2 1

Contents

For Susan Buckley and Robert Mellman

THE LAW OF RETURN

I

The Negroes might march straight up South Orange Avenue and burn the houses to the ground. Our new neighbors would be beaten to a pulp or stabbed into smithereens; their daughters and wives would be ravaged. These were stockbrokers and analysts and corporate executives, men who earned hefty salaries by keeping their eyes on the future. But none of them had expected the flames that roared through Newark's Central Ward three summers earlier. And no one now felt able to predict the next thing that could happen.

For advice and assurance, they went to my father. Every night that summer until my sister returned from Europe, they would glance up from their built-in grills and see him coming in his new Electra, with the top down. In their plaid Bermudas and golf shorts, they crossed their lawns to greet him, sometimes with a frosty glass of gin in hand. He got out of the black convertible with a Macanudo in his mouth, the *Newark News* under one arm and the *Star-Ledger* under the other, a stack of cigar boxes between his big hands. On top were two boxes of pennies and silver, then a box filled with small bills. The bottom box held twenties and fifties, maybe a C-note or two.

But my father could have been carrying the Bible or an entire *Encyclopedia Britannica* and his relative authority wouldn't have increased. In moving to Short Hills, he became an expert—the ordinary truths that he had known for years were suddenly exotica. By the time he reached the edge of our property, the men would be gathered, awaiting his words. Moses himself did not have as attentive an audience when he descended Mt. Sinai; no one, really, likes to listen to someone who must lower himself to deliver pronouncements. But anyone could see the vertical arrow of sweat still staining the back of my father's short-sleeved white shirt.

"Evening, Vic," the neighbor men would say. "How are things down in the jungle? Are the natives growing restless again?"

What could he have answered? How could he explain the facts and nuances? The mysteries of the universe aren't meted out like stock tips. And he must have been flattered. Here he was, at long last ensconced in Jersey's richest town, with a mortgage as large as any of theirs—but still, "a working stiff." He had never drawn a salary that stayed steady whether business was booming or whether it slumped. If business was good, then he gave his guys raises before they could ask; he wouldn't admit it now, but my sister's trip to Europe was originally his idea. If business was bad, then he helped my mother's brother with his concessions, and cut most of his guys' hours. But never Sherman Carter's. He and Sherman might even pour half the pricey Scotches into gallon jugs to use straight again when things picked up. In the meantime, they mixed cheaper brands with what remained. Sherman set a bottle of the married Black & White on the bar and linked arms with my father. They pointed at each other's faces. "He's black," said Sherman. "Like his car." "He's white," said Pop. "Like his."

At night, their pair broke up. Sherman walked around the corner to his two-family house and my father set the cigar boxes on our lawn, careful to avoid the nearest sprinkler system. Only twenty minutes after leaving the Central Ward, he was surrounded by sycamore, cypress, and elm. A cooling breeze dried the sweat from his shirt. The only sound came from little Melanie Bauer, practicing her harp at her opened window. The only smells were of roses and rhododendron, maybe some lighter fluid still wafting.

"Status quo," he told the gathered men. "Just the usual"—he paused, wanting to say *tsuris*, trouble, but settled diplomatically on the nearest English—"aggravation."

The men nodded and leaned forward, as if to savor Cronkite's insights on a breaking story. "It's the kids," he told them. "The old-timers don't give any trouble. Never did. But the kids."

A sigh went up around him. Ice cubes clicked at crystal tumblers. Someone plucked a tuft of grass and chewed it. This was language any man could understand, a kind of Esperanto. They shook their heads, and murmured, and thought about their own confounding offspring, a generation born to disappoint, infuriate. Clem Bauer's older daughter was living in a commune in Vermont. Will Bristol's boy had burned his draft card. Tom Firth's had fled to Canada.

What on earth could happen next?

"I honestly don't know," my father said. "I wouldn't bet my life one way or the other. I've never been a gambler. Not in the true sense of the word."

When he came into the house, I kissed him as he shook his head, looking out the picture window in the living room. He didn't seem to see the slice of moon, the first few stars. He pulled the Macanudo from his mouth. Its tip was soggy green.

"Lillian, can you believe those guys?"

Suddenly he blinked, remembering: my mother was in Miami Beach; my grandfather had had another stroke, his third.

So back to me.

"Smith & Jones"—his collective euphemism for the Short Hills seekers—"can keep their pensions and their paid vacations, seeing as they're pros at the bend and shuffle. But listen to me, Debbie. You'll never catch me kneeling at the feet of another man. Say, did I ever tell you about Mulberry Street?"

That was where he and his mother had lived above a strip-tease joint after his father keeled over dead at the wheel of a Sealtest milk truck. During the day, the strip joint served food, and I could have described, in perfect detail, the aromatic subtleties of pork butt, ham hocks, pigs' knuckles, although I had never tasted any of that.

"Even then, Mulberry was entirely *shvartzer*," said my father. "Unless I held a mirror to my own face, I could walk a mile until I saw a white one. Smith & Jones, they want some insight into how the Negro thinks? Let them pay me a commission. But if I ever asked for what was due, then you can bet they'd say, 'Ain't that just like a kike?' Without the 'ain't', of course."

When I winced, he held my face between his palms and looked into my eyes. "You don't like to hear that, Sweetheart. I don't blame you. How was camp?"

"Oh, Pop. Don't say it like that. Please."

"So sensitive! Like what?"

"'How was camp.' As if I'm a little Leni Lenapan, carrying a lunch box that my mother packed, making boxes out of Elmer's glue and

Popsicle sticks. I'm seventeen."

I was waiting for the summer to be over and my senior year to start. Until then, I was a counselor at my old day camp, up by Lake Hopatcong in the Watchung Mountains.

My father turned from the window and gazed at the living room furniture: a black and white cut velvet couch, two rose loveseats by the marble fireplace that we never lit, a curio cabinet filled with porcelain figurines. We'd been living here three years. Mostly everything was new, different than our house in Newark. The living room seemed wildly misnamed; none of us ever used it. After a moment, my father and I stepped back into the hall.

"These days everybody's raw when it comes to what you call them." My father sighed. "Of course you're not a camper. You're a working girl. And you know how glad that makes me."

"I'm glad that I don't have camp tomorrow."

"A day off is good from time to time. I'm the first one to admit it."

"I'm not taking a day off," I told him. "Tomorrow's Saturday. I'm picking up Marlene at five. I'm using Mama's car. Remember?"

"Of course I remember. Like it or not, she's my daughter, too."

"*Pop.*"

He reached into his pocket and pulled out the ring that held his car keys, slipped off two keys and placed them in my palm.

"Here you go, sweetheart. Live it up—impress your friends. P.S.: I meant that *she's* the one who doesn't like it."

The keys were brass, as bright as gold. "The Electra? Pop, don't tease."

"I'm on the level." In a musing tone he added, "I don't know what I was thinking anyway, driving that car down there. But when it comes to Smith & Jones, you can bet your life on one thing. I'd be the last guy in the world to let them think they had the picture all along. I wouldn't give them the satisfaction." With one hand on the banister, a foot on the next stair, he added, "Anyway, the truth is, Sweetheart, a car is just a car: a vehicle that takes a man from one point to the other. You don't believe that now, but eventually you'll see it."

At the top of the stairs, he called back down. "Meanwhile, enjoy."

My sister was twenty that summer, done with her sophomore year at the University of Wisconsin. In June, she came home for two weeks, and then flew Air Icelandic to Luxembourg with Paula

Eisenberg, whose family had moved from Newark to a West Orange split-level. By early August, Marlene had spent six weeks hitching around Europe with a million other American kids. "But who's counting?" my father liked to say.

He was. A million and *one* were out there on the cobbled streets of ancient cities with their thumbs raised, thronging village lanes and German autobahns—with their rainbows and their peace signs stitched onto their backpacks.

The extra one was Howie Marcus, Marlene's boyfriend. She sent weekly postcards, and, from what I calculated, by early August she had slept with him in six foreign capitols and along the North Sea, the Mediterranean, the Adriatic. They'd met up in Amsterdam. And Paula's boyfriend had been waiting, as agreed, in Copenhagen.

I was pretty sure that my father suspected. "She's widening her horizons. She's seeing the sights with a fine group of young people," he wrote my maternal grandparents in Miami Beach. "She's gallivanting around," was how he described her exploits to the neighbor men. "It could be worse. She could be a pregnant hippie." He caught himself, remembering Clem Bauer's older daughter. "Tramping around" was what he scowled at my mother, later.

Freshman year, Howie had bestowed his AEPi pin on Marlene, and for a while, she wore it proudly on her shetland sweater, just above her heart. That December, after she and Howie watched the national lottery on TV, they agreed to toss the pin into Lake Mendota, along with his draft card and her bra. Howie had drawn a number in the low 300's; a boy couldn't get much safer. But Marlene said it was important that he make a statement.

One month later, my father was eating brisket while he scanned the campus paper that was routinely mailed to parents. I was counting the change from his cigar boxes into stacks of fifty. I took one of the bank's paper wrappers—pink for pennies, blue for nickels, green for dimes—and slipped the tip of a finger inside it. With my other hand I slid in the stack of coins, tamped the filled tube on the kitchen table until the wrapper snugly fit, then folded in both ends. My father handled the counting and stacking of the bills. Later, I would do the totals on the adding machine while he did them in his head. I never once had finished first or caught him in an error.

I was reaching for the box of quarters when he turned a page and saw my sister's photograph. She and Howie were standing on the steps of the Wisconsin state capitol. People thronged the streets as far as could be seen, but somehow the photographer had closed in on Marlene and her boyfriend—her "paramour," my father called him. She was hoisting a sign tacked to a wooden stake and Howie's fist was raised. According to the caption, he had spent the night in jail.

"That's it. I've had it," Pop announced. "That's the last straw. Marlene can just come home and go to Montclair State. Or Douglass, if Montclair's too close for comfort. There's nothing wrong with Douglass."

"That's enough with the salt," my mother told him, and yanked the shaker from his hand. He always salted first and tasted second, and she always had to watch him. "Do you realize what you're doing to your pressure?"

"What *I'm* doing to it? That's rich."

He got up, grabbed a cigar from the humidor and a nectarine from the refrigerator, and stomped into the yard. Beyond the glass sliders were a cobblestone patio and an area of lawn; then came a formal rock garden, bisected by a narrow path sloping up a small hill. The previous owners had hired a landscape architect to arrange those odd piles of stone, apparently intending to simulate an outdoor terrarium. But as soon as we moved in, my parents had asked an electrician to install a dozen bronze fish and frogs along the path. Small safety beacons lit the way from inside their gaping mouths. "I don't want any lawsuits if some rich kid trips and breaks his neck out there," my father said.

Now he bent to fiddle with each one of the safety lights. By the time he seemed sure they all were working, his Macanudo had gone out. He tossed the nectarine pit at the rock garden, struck a match, and cupped his hands around the flame. He couldn't get the stub relit, so finally, he tossed that out there, too.

II

The Electra was a teenager's dream. It had big whitewalls and pointed fins, a nubbed black canvas roof, and a fine vibrant smell that I imagined to be leather, but which must have been top-grade vinyl. My father hadn't especially needed a new car, but business had been booming at his tavern since the riots, just as he predicted on the night that Newark burned, and so he traded in his old convertible and bought a fancier one.

In the morning, I fixed us some salami and eggs, not too dry—the way he liked them—and we ate our breakfast on the patio while we shared the morning's *Ledger*. The heat had started early and seemed to shimmer like chiffon above the grass. My father was in a white shirt and white pants. I wore a new striped halter dress. I don't recall our conversation, or if we talked at all, or what the headlines might have been—the latest casualties in Vietnam? The latest protest marches? That morning, I thought only of driving the Electra with the top down, the hot breeze in my hair, the sun massaging my bare shoulders. So I cannot know if he was thinking of Marlene and the first thing he would say to her, the way I often planned for days the first words I would utter if a boy like Jimmy Noh approached me. He might have been. It was a Saturday, the tavern's busiest time; my father wouldn't have a chance to think a single thought once things there started "hopping." He'd get home long past midnight. She'd be tired from the flight, he'd be tired from the night, and with any luck at all they could greet each other gladly, maybe even manage until Labor Day, when she flew back to Madison.

He dawdled, full of compliments on the orange juice I'd squeezed by hand, and didn't leave the house until a little after ten. He was headed to the new Y on Northfield Avenue for a dose of steam, then over to his barber for his weekly trim before he went to work. He wasn't gone ten minutes when my mother called from Florida, reporting on my grandfather's health—he had lost his speech but would survive; his spirits seemed quite good, although of course she couldn't be certain—and reminding me my sister's flight was due that afternoon, as if I could forget. She seemed pleased for me about the chance to drive the Electra. But when I said that switching cars had been my father's idea, not mine, I heard something in her tone that usually didn't surface: a flinch of breath, an extra beat, another detail that might have given pause if I hadn't been enmeshed in visions of my debut drive. I sent my love to both my grandparents, even if Gramp couldn't send his back—at least this much of her message made its way into my consciousness—and promised to have Marlene call them all that night. Then I dialed the few girls I knew me was that everyone, including my own parents, was applauding. And my sister started laughing. When they turned my way to smile, I started screaming. My mother had to bring me to the Ladies' Room and splash cold water on my face and neck. She explained what we had seen, but I didn't believe her. I thought for sure the maitre'd and waiter planned to kill us all.

Nowadays, it's different. Route 22 is crumbling, only used for local traffic. Both sides of Route 24's eight lanes are walled with massive concrete, like an endless roofless bunker. International flights take off frequently from the newer, grander terminals and The Newarker, of course, is gone. I doubt that buses filled with school-children still take field trips to the gray and rather squat control tower I passed that afternoon, or are told that nowhere—not in Paris, London, Rome, or Amsterdam—could another one be taller or more ideally placed to assure our safety. The giant traffic cloverleaf connecting the airport to Route 24 is elevated, so that travelers never have to see the city that remains below.

But even then, I didn't really see it, either—just some camouflaging greenery along its edges, and the black nose of the Electra, and my forearms browning in the sun.

In the crowded waiting area, exasperated adults sprawled on splintered benches, babies howled in their carriages, crew-cut customs agents slouched against their stations. Everybody steamed, impatient for the vagabonds. Through a streaked glass wall, I watched my sister hand her passport to a customs agent. She was wearing blue jeans and a gauzy off-the-shoulders peasant blouse, embroidered at the yoke in brilliant blues and reds. As the agent made a lazy show of rifling her things he chatted amiably, watching with great interest as she reached behind her neck and hooked her heavy auburn hair in place with a sort of leather stick.

At a customs station several lanes away, another agent fingered Howie's guidebooks, shook his underwear for contraband, and fiddled with the harmonica that Howie carried everywhere. Howie had to make a connecting flight to Chicago, where his parents lived. He wore an army jungle outfit. His hair reached to his shoulders. He kept glancing at the clock on the wall until finally, with a grudging nod, the agent waved him through. It took several minutes longer for Howie to gather his things and shove them in his back-pack. He called out to Marlene, and she pressed two fingers to her lips, then waved them Howie's way. The agent stamped her passport, and she, too, was free.

In another minute, we were hugging. She felt thinner in my arms than I remembered, but more solid—she had been trekking for six weeks. She laughed and shook me back, my elbows in her palms.

"Debbie-Ebby, I think you've grown again. But for God's sake, are you still setting your hair on those awful metal rollers?"

I was, of course. "I'll stop," I said as she held out her back-pack. I took the top of the frame, she took the bottom and we started walking toward the exit.

"That guy seemed to really like you," I said.

"But of course, *ma cherie*. And I love him."

I motioned back toward the customs area. "Not Howie. I meant the guy in there who checked you through. Him," I told her, pointing.

"*Him?*"

She shrugged and we kept walking. "Oh, sure. Guys like that think girls like me are easy lays. Look." She snapped the elasticized neckline of her peasant blouse. "No bra. *Ergo*: slut. And when it comes to guys like Howie, forget it altogether. I'm surprised they didn't make him strip, so they could get their rocks off. Those fascists do it all the time."

She had brought me a lacy black mantilla, dappled with small silver discs, and a box of writing paper. The paper was marbleized in shades of green and softly frayed around the edges, nearly beige; it had the silky feel of the oldest bills my father counted at our kitchen table, smooth and strong as fabric. In the car, I held the first sheet at the hot air and was astonished to see there an entire scene: a stone clock tower with a sun and moon visible on its face, men in Renaissance dress pushing horse-drawn carts, women bargaining with shopkeepers.

"It's from this old Italian hill town," said Marlene. "They still make that paper by hand. I guess the clock-tower used to be in the main piazza. They used it as a look-out."

But it was the mantilla that I really loved. I draped the silvery netting on my head and across my sunburned shoulders, studying myself in the rear-view mirror. I didn't look too skinny now. I looked virginal yet mature, a young beauty tragically widowed before the consummation of her wedding vows, and devoted to the image of what might have been.

In the rear-view mirror, a jet broke the sky and roared, billowing the clouds. I could barely hear Marlene until she shouted.

"I tried to get you something from Amsterdam because that was my favorite place. But I couldn't exactly bring you back a bit of hash. These days the airports are crawling with pigs."

"*God,* Marlene." I had eased out of the parking lot, down the Van Wyck Expressway, and was headed to the Verrazano Bridge. I had always wanted to drive across the Verrazano but hadn't had the nerve to try alone. The bridge was less than ten years old then and gleamed across the Narrows like a giant tiara. In the sparkling water, steamships headed out for parts unknown.

"Don't worry," Marlene said as we shot across Staten Island, toward the Goethals Bridge and into Jersey. From the port city of Elizabeth, I planned to take Morris Avenue up to Union and over to Short Hills. "I wouldn't try bringing hash back here, believe me."

A huge truck roared by and I felt the mantilla loosen. But the Electra didn't shimmy an inch. "Shhh," I said, then laughed at my own caution. Nobody could hear her words above the wind.

We had reached the corner of Morris and Elmora. I flicked on my directional and, as I'd been taught in Driver's Ed, signaled left with my hand.

"Don't turn," Marlene said. "We'll cut through Hillside and take a look at Newark."

"I don't think we should," I told her. "I don't think Pop would like it."

"We'll stop in at the place and surprise him. We can put the top up if you'll feel better." She pressed her finger to the button on the dashboard and the roof began to lift. "I never really understood why he bought this car," she added. "It's kind of ostentatious."

"This is an Electra," I protested. "It's the top of the line."

She laughed and snapped the top of the roof into place.

"Jesus," she said.

We were driving down a block that looked as if it had burned the day before instead of three years earlier. The storefronts were chipped foundations, the sidewalks strewn with charred and splintered planks, with mountains of glass shards that caught the fading sun. Some of the trees along the curb were scorched and blackened. The edges of the stop signs had melted into curves; here and there a few wildflowers struggled through the rubble.

"This looks worse than the worst part of Marrakech," Marlene said.

On the next block, a clutch of yellow saw-horses stamped, "NEWARK POLICE—DO NOT MOVE" made a jagged cautionary jail of several wooden houses in danger of collapsing. Faded and decaying, the sawhorses had probably stood guard there since the first match in the riots had been struck. And then the second match was struck, the third, a dozen or a hundred, and the Central Ward erupted. I tried to imagine how it must have looked that night: the flames that reached as high as towers, the men and women running to be safe. And the youngest children shrieking—with fear? Or, not yet knowing what they saw, with pleasure?

My sister's voice was calm, objective. "Marrakech is poorer, probably, but at least it's warm and sunny there," she said.

By then, I must have been quite flushed. She glanced at my face and took a Wash-an'-Dri from the compartment as I turned down a quiet street that seemed as if it hadn't ever seen the flames. But this one was most eerie-physically intact but empty now of something, as if, through sheer will or simple luck, the street had managed to survive the riots, but then caught the inflammation anyway. Marlene bit open the wrapper on the moist towelette and wiped my neck.

"It's warm and sunny here," I said when she was done. "If the top was down, you'd feel it stronger."

But by then, she had turned back to her window, and was talking on about the slums of Lisbon, the drab working-class sections of London, the squatters in West Berlin and the hovels in Paris where the Algerians were forced to live. I wondered if she was exhausted from the long flight back, or from wandering the more magnificent ruins at Athens and Pompeii. Perhaps she meant to teach me something that she thought I hadn't learned, or might not believe.

But as the red sun lowered toward the Orange Mountains, it seemed to me she might have been reciting from a travel brochure composed by someone well-intended but distant from the scene.

The Law of Return

My father wasn't at the place when we stopped in there. I left the Electra near the intersection, at what was once Kaminsky's Corner Mart, but didn't see my mother's blue sedan anywhere along the street. During the riots, Mr. Kaminsky had shot himself in the ankle while he was trying to figure out his gun and never reopened his store. My father had his billyclub, and at the time, my mother thought that Sherman Carter might have had a knife, but later, both men said that they were lucky neither one wound up like Moe Kaminsky. They said that they had never been in danger anyway, except maybe from the National Guard, because the fires never reached their way. And except for the occasional marrying of Scotches, their customers had no beef with them.

One of the guys who helped them out those nights was at the taps, flicking streams of Bud and Rheingold into frosted mugs, when Marlene and I walked in. Another fixed mixed drinks and poured the shots. Sherman covered the register, which was set in the middle of the bar so he could watch both ways. Unframed mirrors, smoky blue and veined with silver, hung on every wall; nothing passed his notice. Every drink was paid for as soon as it was ordered. "At The Newarker they let a guy run up a tab," my father often said. "I don't own The Newarker."

Sherman greeted us and leaned across the bar to ask Marlene about her trip. Above the throbbing music on the juke-box, the whack of cue sticks and exploding pool balls, she tried to tell him various highlights—Big Ben, the Eiffel Tower, the canals and palaces of Venice. A few couples sat at tables covered in red oilcloth, but most stood pressed together, sometimes because there simply was no other place to be and sometimes, from the way they laughed and flirted, because they seemed to like the brush against another body on a steamy summer evening. I didn't feel quite myself as I stood watching. I felt too tall and gangly, exposed in my striped halter dress. I knew half the customers by name and several more by sight, but that night I felt as if they all, especially the ones I didn't know, were staring at me—with indulgence, even tolerance, not hostility. But the more they smiled in my direction, the more uncomfortable I felt. The customers I didn't know must have wondered who we were, what we were doing in that place. Eventually, somebody would tell them we were Vic Tarlow's daughters. But who else could we have been? I asked Sherman where he was.

"Vic took off early." The register sang open. Sherman's fingers on the ivory keys were swift and graceful as a pianist's, but his eyes stayed steady on the scene ahead. "First time I've seen that happen. Your father figured he'd surprise Marlene."

III

It was nearly nine o'clock when I turned past the Congregational Church, down Parsonage Hill, onto our street. My father was standing on our lawn without his usual stack of cigar boxes, but surrounded by his usual acolytes. He must have passed out Macanudos. Centered in the gathered men, his face was barely visible, masked by the rich smoke. But when it cleared, I knew immediately from his expression that we should have come straight home. And I realized why the tavern's customers had been staring. I was still wearing the silvery mantilla Marlene had brought me.

I pulled into the driveway and whipped it off, not quite fast enough.

"What the hell was that old *shmatta* on your head?" he said when he came over. Marlene still had a hand on the door of the Electra. "Don't you have a decent sunhat? Didn't your mother buy one for you just last week at Lord & Taylor?"

"Marlene brought it back for me from Portugal. It's a mantilla. Widows wear them."

"With all that silver hoopla on it?"

"Spain," she said. "We never got to Portugal. We meant to, but the time ran out. Hi, Pop."

She walked around the car and kissed him. That seemed to calm him, or else he looked across the lawn and saw the men still gathered.

"The World Traveler has returned," he boomed. "She ran out of time, not money. Can you beat that? Kids!" He put an arm around her shoulder and, with a nod, dismissed them. As the men dispersed he dropped his arm, turned my way, and held out his palm.

"Give me the keys," he said.

I had them ready, knowing he would ask. "I'm sorry, Pop," I told him.

"For what?" Marlene seemed genuinely puzzled. "She drove great, Pop. She's really careful. She's ten times better than I was when I started."

He hooked the keys back on his ring and cocked his head, then pulled his Macanudo from his mouth and twirled it. "You don't say."

"She's a terrific driver," Marlene insisted. "She didn't do one thing wrong. I was watching the whole time."

"Let's go in," I said. "Why stand out here? We'll get eaten up alive by the mosquitoes. Come on, I'll fix iced tea. We can call Mama in Miami Beach," I added feebly.

"She called a little while ago." My father's voice was absolutely flat. "I had to tell her that you'd both been killed. I wasn't sure if Marlene's plane went up in flames, or if maybe she'd crashed in a cab or a bus going to the airport—are there cabs in Luxembourg? Or do they have those big red buses? No, no, I'm thinking London. Anyway, I told your mother that for sure you, Deborah Ann, had been killed in the Electra. I said to her: 'There's no doubt about it. I never should have bought that car.'"

"For God's sake," said Marlene.

I started inching up the walk, knowing he would have to follow. She hoisted on her back-pack and came after. "I thought you had enough sense to drive straight home," he told me. "I thought you'd realize I would worry."

I got them both inside. Marlene shrugged her back-pack into the corner of the foyer and walked into the kitchen. We heard the refrigerator open and then we heard it slam. The air-conditioning was way too cold and I started shivering from my sun-burn. "I know," I said. "I'm sorry, Pop. We thought you wouldn't be home until later."

"We stopped by the place," Marlene called out.

He turned, and with his eyes asked if this was true. I nodded, looking at the carpet. Then I followed as he walked into the kitchen.

She was sitting at the table, sipping Hoffman's Black Cherry from the bottle.

"We wanted to surprise you," she told him.

"You," he said. "Not her. You wanted."

With the back of her hand, she wiped the soda from her lips and watched his face. "Well, I'm the one who's been away. I'm the one who hasn't seen you."

"She's seventeen years old. But you—you're all of a hot twenty.

So you, at least, being a hot twenty, should have the smarts to figure out a thing or two. For instance. The Central Ward's a dangerous place these days. Two young girls, a brand-new convertible: don't you know what could have happened?"

"What could happen?" said Marlene.

He imitated her, in a simpering voice that wasn't fair. "'What could happen?'" Then he shrugged—again, a shrug that wasn't hers or his either, but the movement of a stranger, no one who I knew. I watched him with a mix of fear and fascination. It was as if he had a talent, or a defect, I had never noticed.

"Did you spend the summer smoking reefer? Didn't you once come up for air? And to top it off you had to make her wear that trashy get-up? Why didn't you just glue dollar bills across her forehead? *What could have happened?* To you it's probably nothing anyway. Nothing that you haven't already done."

"Pop, don't," I said. But I doubt he even heard me. By then his skin was red, his eyes were huge.

I went to the sliding doors and pressed my burning face against the glass. Outside, two robins sat motionless on the head of a bronze frog.

"What exactly do you mean?" Marlene said in an even voice, behind me.

"You know, 'exactly,' what I mean."

"I don't."

"But you're a college girl. I shouldn't have to spell it out."

"Tell me what you mean."

"I mean that you've been shacking up for six weeks with your long-haired boyfriend, and I'm sick of standing on my feet ten hours a day down in the jungle so you can act 'exactly' like a slut! That's 'exactly' what I mean!"

I turned, and saw by his expression that he knew. Right then, he knew exactly how terrible were the things he had said, how incendiary. And he must have also known that one moment, maybe two or three, still remained to take them back, to douse them.

But he didn't. The moments passed. And then my sister set down the Hoffman's and stood to face him.

"If I'm a slut, then you—then you're a slum-lord!"

It happened just like that, the same way fire starts: small, not much, a match or two, and then the leap straight toward the sky.

The Law of Return

It would seem as if what happened next should appear to me in fine detail, in perfect focus. In memory, each footstep should be recognizable, each sound of my father's or my sister's as particular as a face, a voice, a kiss. My bedroom was just off the stairwell. The house was relatively new. Although a well-known architect designed it, most sounds traveled easily. Interpreting whose steps were whose had always been the simplest task, one in which I took a certain pride. So it seems I should recall who first left the house that night and who went where.

But of course, that is not how memory operates. All I know for certain is that both were in their rooms, both doors were shut, when at last I got upstairs; I must have killed some time in the kitchen—doing what, I can't imagine—once they vanished. I shut my door, relieved to be away from both of them, and hoped with greater fervor than I'd ever hoped for anything that they would stay in their respective caves forever. I spread the marbleized Italian paper on my desk and started writing something. Probably a letter. But to whom? It must have been to my grandfather, struggling in Miami Beach to learn again how to move his toes and fingers, to make his lips form sounds. But he spoke no English and I knew scarcely any Yiddish; in the best of times, we mostly held each other's hands and smiled.

Still, I don't know who else I might have written. Those girlfriends who'd gone off to "summer" soon would be returning. And, in any case, I wouldn't have scribbled any family difficulties to them. Nor would they have written me of similar troubles. Under cover of a civility that seemed essential to survival, my mother and the neighbor women might discuss vacation spots; my father and the men might trade financial forecasts. But such tactics were, at best, diversionary. The secrecy and cover-ups that my sister and her college friends railed against and often protested seem, in retrospect, a natural extension of our own domestic policies.

I do recall that by the time my careful script had covered half the paper's watermark, darkening half the clock tower and half the Renaissance townspeople, one of them and then the other made the trip downstairs. Then up a while later, then down again. Did they glimpse or even pass each other inadvertently—but pretend they didn't see or recognize anything familiar in the other's face? Convince themselves that they were members of entirely different species, rather than such similar flesh and bone? They must have, and retreated, then kept going. I went out to the guest room, turned the volume on the television as high as it would go, and closed the door behind me so they would think that I was in there focused on the noisy screen. I went back into my room and in a while I managed to ignore them, as if I were not affected in the least, as if I needed nothing from them, not the simplest civility nor instruction nor assurance. I sat at my desk with my door closed, my eyes aimed at the green paper, veering from the simplest English phrases to those few errant Yiddish words I knew, and I tried to find a way to tell my grandfather what had happened without adding to his troubles. I pretended that my father and my sister were foreigners, from a rival tribe or city-state; through no transgression of my own, but due to a series of irrational decisions in which I had no say, they somehow had been granted residence in the exact same place as I. But that didn't mean I had to see them—her, or him.

Eventually, I got up from my desk and went to my window. The moon was nearly full that night. The entire yard seemed lit. My sister stood in the middle of the rock garden, tossing stones uphill, watching them come down. She knelt and chose another stone, tossed it up and knelt again. She performed these simple actions without apparent anger or aggression, but with a rhythmic grace, in what seemed a kind of trance, an urge her body had for movement, even preservation, which she couldn't help but obey. She had changed from her peasant blouse and jeans into an old house dress of my mother's. And that still surprises me. Because for a long time afterwards, thinking back upon that night, I seemed to see my father standing in his work clothes among the bronze frogs and fish. In truth, he wasn't in the yard, or even near it—but, still, I seem to see him standing there, not moving, scarcely breathing. Sometimes, I even think there may be time to go downstairs and say something to him. But I never can imagine what I might have said, or what he might have answered.

It was probably near midnight by the time I heard his footsteps on the stairs again. The staircase ended near the kitchen and the sliders that Marlene had left open. I would have heard his first few steps and she'd have heard him reach the bottom. When I saw her walk across the yard to watch, I went to my other window. He got into the convertible and backed out of the driveway, then headed toward the Congregational Church and Parsonage Hill, his standard route to and from the tavern. Where else could he have gone? He returned to what was most familiar, the place where he felt safest.

And this, above all else that happened next, remains the clearest detail and the one I most regret: it was the Electra, not my father, that I hated to see leaving.

He was shot, not fatally, two hours later that same night. He was shot once and then again, two bullets fired in quick succession. But in the future, his flesh would show three separate holes.

The first bullet ripped into his upper arm and exited the other side. It left a pucker of gray-green flesh about the size of a dime going in, a nickel as it came out. When the surgeons emerged from the operating room at the Beth Israel, down in Newark, the head man had it fisted in his palm. He splayed his fingers to reveal the bloodied silver and I felt like kneeling at his feet. He tried to give it to my mother but she didn't want it, didn't even want to touch it.

That third hole, the hole in his gut, I never saw. He was far too modest a man to reveal it, even prostrate in his bed, all doped up. But my mother told me it was bigger than a quarter. He couldn't conceal the holes in his right arm because first the nurses, then she herself, had to regularly shave from his knuckles to his shoulder and cut the sleeve from his pajamas so the bandages could fit. Once, when she was exhausted, we worried she might slash him. My sister took the razor and drew the curtain on its ceiling track around his bed, so even then I couldn't see. She must have also shaved his gut, the mat of dark brown hair that nearly camouflaged the skin. By then, he had started speaking—one word here or there. Although I thought he would demand some sleeves to hide the evidence of his shame, he didn't.

He demanded nothing and asked for nothing in the long weeks of his recuperation. He watched the hands that worked on him, and the movements of the mouths that offered their professional advice, in silence. Later, he listened to Dr. Rabinowitz pleading that he really was alright now; he should put it behind him and go forward. Go on a vacation. My father watched and heard each of those who tended him with his big, pale face as blank and lifeless as a city block just razed, a fine old building gutted. He didn't argue with the nurses or the doctors, not one word in contradiction, or with my mother, either.

The day after he was shot, she had come flying into Intensive Care from her father's bed at Sinai in Miami to his at the Beth Israel, the cabby right beside her. Out on Lyons Avenue, the meter still was running. It was a hefty fare from Newark Airport and the cabbie was sorry, at a time like this, but he just wanted what was due. The cabby might have been a dead man; my mother pushed straight past him to the doctors. Marlene took him out into the hall and paid him.

At home, in the guest room, we had a new TV set with remote control. Weeks later, when my mother stood repeating what the doctors said, my father watched her with the same blank face, the clicker in mid-air. Late one night, she started screaming. It was one thing for my grandfather to be silent, frozen by his third stroke even out of Yiddish! It was another thing entirely for my father to lie there giving homage to some ancient fantasy that he was nearly Negro, when all along, and especially since the riots, she had warned that this could happen. She had asked him to get out, she had begged him to get out; Rabinowitz had urged him—even Sherman Carter, even Sherman tried to tell him, even Sherman knew he should get out!

Eventually, she threw the razor at the wall, and, in silence, he clicked to the next channel. If, during the remaining weeks of that summer, he had seen himself reflected in a mirror, he wouldn't have recognized the man in bed, the one who wouldn't react. For he had behaved altogether differently on the night the three punks shot him, as if he were another man entirely, still young and vigorous and strong: self-righteous, almost. He couldn't have realized then that one era was about to end, another to begin.

He and Sherman closed the place a little after two o'clock. Sherman sorted the cash into the cigar boxes lined up on the bar—pennies and nickels first, then dimes and quarters, the next with ones and fives, the penultimate with tens and twenties, the last box filled with fifties and two C-notes. The cash register itself was worth enough that, as usual, my father left the final C-note in it with the drawer wide open: if the place was broken into, which had often happened, the thieves wouldn't need to damage it. With his key ring dangling from his fingers, he stacked the cigar boxes—high denominations on the bottom, low on top—and the two men walked outside. For a while, they stood together on the sidewalk, where they had stood guard together in the riots. They talked: perhaps about a customer who'd been banned for nearly fighting, or about the next week's schedule, or maybe Sherman's kids—not Marlene or even me, I'm certain. They might have talked about the weather, the off-chance that the heat might break. About this latter possibility, they shared mixed feelings. The temperature was unbearable, but this had been an exceptionally good night, in terms of business; the heat kept people drinking. They said good-bye and Sherman walked straight home. My father crossed the street.

I wonder if he broke his own law then and lingered? Stood alone with his cigar boxes on that street not far from Mulberry and, loathe to face the next day with my sister, gave too long a moment to remembering his past, to history, instead of looking forward? To the image of his father hunched over in the Sealtest truck with his immigrant heart completely shot from too much working, too much dreaming? To his mother, not much longer for this world, either, taking in the wash of strangers to keep the two of them afloat, always wishing they could move back from their single room above the strip joint to the rooms they'd had above a pickler in another poor, but Jewish, section of the city? To the strip-tease joint itself, and the lessons he had learned while racing to move up from it?

When the three punks jumped out from what remained of Kaminsky's Corner Mart, my father saw them coming in the moonlight. He knew immediately what they were after. It wasn't hard to figure. All three kids' foreheads, hands and chests dripped sweat. Their eyes were glazed, unseeing. It was clear that they were junkies. He almost started laughing at the youngest, who was nearly nodding off as he asked for the stacked boxes in a voice still high and boyish, not a man's. It wasn't that my father didn't see or hear. It wasn't that his senses had stopped working. He stood on that forsaken street and saw the gun that glinted from a sweating palm. He heard what the punks were saying. But it was his turf that they tried to take, his place that they violated. Over his dead body.

They scuffled. The youngest one ran off. My father's power must have stunned the other two. He felt his fist smash at a face, then at another. The junkies swayed and staggered—if there had been music, a passing stranger would have thought the pair were dancing. Just before they turned to run, the tallest grabbed the top two boxes. And my father chased him. But I have never known, and he never could remember, what he did with the remaining boxes when he ran. Did he set them on the broken sidewalk as carefully as he set them on the manicured lawn when speaking to his followers in the suburbs? Why would he carry into battle precisely what he sought so desperately to protect? For that matter: how could he have wielded his clenched fists with both arms full? Yet he swore he never put the boxes down.

He ran straight at them. He wasn't ten feet off when the tallest punk, who held the gun, yelled out to the others: "This old honky's crazy." Two bursts of bluish gunfire lit the night.

They didn't know him, Sherman tried to tell him later. Not by name or even sight. They were kids he had never seen before and never would again. They weren't from the neighborhood. They didn't belong there. They might as well have been raised up in some wild, distant country. They might as well have been raised up in Short Hills! For the first time since that night, my father smiled.

Anyway, said Sherman, they weren't merely kids. No decent person's kids could do what they did. They were junkies, pure and simple, young desperadoes hooked on heroin, staggering like three rabid pups. *They* were the ones who deserved to be shot, put out of their own misery. You could call it anything you wanted, you could make up fancy theories until the day you died to try explaining. But in the end, it was no more and no less than simple luck, the worst luck in the world, that my father was so testy and disorganized that night, so unlike himself when he returned from Short Hills to the Central Ward, he left his own gun underneath the tavern's carved oak bar.

What happened next now seems inevitable. He could have staggered back into the place and called for help. Once inside, he could have called an ambulance or the police, or Sherman, even us. But in the scuffle, he had dropped the key ring for the tavern. Maybe it was somewhere on the sidewalk, or maybe it flew into the curb; either way, he had to get the hell away, get out. The car was closer. And if the cops had come, ostensibly to help him, sure as hell they'd pocket what was in the boxes, then fabricate some bullshit story as a cover-up. Pigs? Marlene, the fancy college girl, thought maybe she could teach him something he had always known deep within his gut, in each bone of his body? For years, he had watched what they could do, he had seen it with his own two eyes! He smelled the fear they spread like fire. For years, he dutifully had paid them off! Every week, a little blood money in a paper bag to leave him and his guys in peace, especially to leave his guys in peace each midnight when they gave up his protection and turned back into *niggers*— indistinguishable in the darkness, the cops told him to his face. He heard them with his own two ears. But he wouldn't call them Pigs in front of either one of us, or let my sister utter such a thing, however true. Never would he do that. For us, he wanted something different.

He made his way toward the Electra bleeding like a bastard, as he later put it, from his upper arm and what appeared to be his stomach. When enough years had passed, he teased my mother that his first thought had been this: At last he'd lose some weight. She and Rabinowitz would finally stop hocking him to diet.

His next thought, the one that kept recurring as he lay in bed for weeks without a word: Gunned down like a dog on his own block for penny-ante stakes, a few nickels and not even dimes.

That night, he nearly passed out from the shame of it. But, by then, he had reached the black Electra. He tried sliding in the cigar boxes, but just opening the goddamned door had been all that he could do. As he leaned across the seat, the boxes hit the dashboard. Their lids flew open, raining bills and silver on the top-grade vinyl. With his good arm, he shoved the whole mess over and somehow dragged his body in behind the wheel. He put the convertible in gear and made his getaway up South Orange Avenue with the brights on, past the Congregational Church, down Parsonage Hill. He worried that he would forget the route, but he didn't. He drove straight onto our lawn and let himself collapse into the horn.

When we got to him, several dollar bills were stuck to the matted hair on his right arm. On his white pants, below the belt, a C-note and a newly minted quarter had been glued by his own blood.

IV

I was walking, late afternoon on Labor Day. No red or orange showed yet, but a few leaves had gone to speckled yellow. All the girls I knew from school were home from wherever they had spent the summer. Down the Jersey shore, in the Hamptons and on Cape Cod, the beaches would be empty, the buildings shuttered.

In our house, everyone had finished packing. My sister's suitcases were stacked in the foyer and her back-pack had gone up to the attic; she was flying to Madison that evening. My parents had booked a flight from Newark for early the next morning. Two plump garment bags were laid out on their bed like a pair of bodies, stuffed with bathing suits and straw hats and suntan lotion. Without a word of argument, my father had agreed to spend a few days in the Virgin Islands. "All I ask," he told my mother of the island of his exile, "is that the joint's American. I don't want to look out every morning on some foreign flag that serves God knows what kind of food."

Right now, he was at the kitchen table, settling the last details with Sherman Carter. Sherman's car sat in our driveway. It wasn't a convertible and it wasn't white exactly, as Sherman always joked when he and Pop linked arms and pretended nobody could tell which man was which, which race was which. It was more of a pale buttery color. My father's car sat next to Sherman's. At the end of August, I had driven it to a guy in Irvington who specialized in stain removal. He spent hours trying to get the blood out of the upholstery, and after his efforts, the front seat looked nearly new. But his miracle didn't matter. My father wouldn't go near the car and my mother said she had never wanted a convertible, anyway. She said it was a car for young people, or people trying to pass for young. That morning, my father had offered Marlene the Electra, but she burst into tears and ran into the yard. He took his coffee out there, and through the sliders, I could see him trying to convince her. But she wouldn't change her mind, so exchanging the convertible for Sherman's car was included in the deal my father struck with him. I didn't know the full terms of the tavern's sale. But he said that it was fair to both of them, and something that he should have done much sooner.

I wasn't going to the Virgin Islands and had been walking for an hour or so. I had always loved the change of season, and still do. Some people—my sister, for instance—find the shifting in the air and light to be funereal and unsettling, inviting lethargy and rumination. But I prefer those times when things begin to change. The boys were back in town now, too. In a half-mile or so I came to Jimmy Noh's house. He was shooting baskets with his brother on the court out by their pool, which was covered in tarpaulin until next summer. *Bong, whoosh. Bong, whoosh.* Jimmy hoped to make the varsity team this year, and I hoped that this would be the year he finally noticed me.

Jimmy lived in a different section of Short Hills, an older one where few Jews had yet staked claims. But my father said this too was now inevitable: that people like the Nohs would soon move further west, to Bernardsville and Far Hills and beyond. For a while, I lingered at the edge of Jimmy's lawn, pretending that I might have lost my way. But, in truth, by then I had come to know the local streets as well as I knew those around Keer Avenue, in Newark. Eventually, I would know them better. It was knowledge I had never wanted and, like my father, had resisted—there were always quicker routes he could have used to and from the Central Ward to shorten what I assumed to be a lonely ride from there to here. But although it drove my mother crazy, he refused to learn them.

I walked back the long way. It was dusk now. The sprinklers had begun their timed rejuvenation of the grass and sculpted hedges. At Parsonage Hill, I stopped and looked across the sloping lawn behind the Congregational Church. I couldn't hear Melanie Bauer's harp, but I could see her strumming at her bedroom window. I could see the neighbor men bent over at their built-in grills, turning franks and flipping burgers for the season's final cook-out. And it occurred to me that this had been precisely the same view to greet my father every night when he drove South Orange Avenue up the mountain from the Central Ward. I always had assumed his pleasure and relief when at last he made his way to us at the end of a long day, but now I saw the watermark: how strange and out of place he must have felt, how much like a tourist, when he suddenly looked out on so much that was foreign.

And Marlene must have felt the same. She had lived in Newark her whole life, but only one year in Short Hills before going off to college. That tension had produced a dangerous simmering that my father must have understood, even as he claimed that it was alien. She had picked a school halfway across one continent and spent her summer on another; he had refused to surrender his last inch of familiar turf. Their tactics had been different, but their struggle wasn't.

Our front door opened and they came out with Sherman Carter, and my mother. In single file, the four of them walked toward the black Electra as the neighbor men glanced up from their backyard grills and moved to their front lawns. They stood there holding metal forks, their hands in quilted mittens, looking toward my father. He must have seen them waiting for a word, but he gave no sign of recognition. In the end, he was a false Messiah, and there was nothing he could say to them.

He turned back to Sherman, my mother and Marlene. And he, or Sherman, must have made a joke, because they started laughing. But I could see the envy on my father's face as the two of them shook hands. Sherman had a Macanudo in his mouth and was carrying the last boxes of my father's private stash, banned forever by the doctors. From the post where I stood watching, I couldn't smell any smoke. But I knew that, in my own way, I would miss it. I walked quickly down the hill to breathe it in, before the missing had to start.

DAYS OF AWE

My grandparents' house didn't look like any of the other houses in Newark's Weequahic section. It looked like a hacienda that belonged in New Mexico or southern California or someplace even stranger. It was made of swirled white stucco, as if massive fingers had swiped at the surface while the stucco was setting, and it sat on a wide steppe of land that dipped between Mapes and Renner Avenues. Manicured cypress hedges and a wrought-iron fence bordered the property all around. At the front entrance, two stone lions on stone pedestals stood guard. From either approach, the green tiled roof was barely visible.

Mapes was a side street; Renner took a bit more traffic. They angled toward each other and crossed at busy Weequahic Avenue, which eventually turned into Broad Street and raced downtown to Market, and the heart of Newark. Even in the heat, with the cypress hedges shriveled up and offering scant protection, a stranger driving past couldn't see the house—which was exactly how my Uncle Nat, who lived there with my grandparents when he wasn't traveling, always wanted things. Nat was the one who had paid cash for the house and everything inside, so he was the one who called the shots. He bought the inlaid rosewood table in the dining room, the chandeliers with sharp-edged crystal pendants, the solarium's imported plants and flowers.

But to me, it was the white brick garage at the top of the driveway that was most exotic: that single, potent image that seems to rest upon the others, invisible but somehow present, as the hand of God is said to rest upon the shoulders of those who are believers.

Inside was shadowed, slightly cooler than the steamy outside air.

As a boy in Czarist Russia, my grandfather had apprenticed to a harness-maker, but in Newark, stunned by the dearth of horses needing hand-wrought gear, he switched to cobbling shoes. Now the garage had the aura common in museums of that era, before museums turned to airy art forms—old and musty places, sad. Near the single window on the far wall was a pile of soft green folded felts belonging to my uncle. On top of the felts lay the rusted awl and chisel that my grandfather had carried with his prayer books on the boat to Ellis Island, and the stately oak hammer so heavy that its heft bent back my wrist when I held it. Nearby, on a splintered wooden bench, sat the only saddle that he ever stitched in Newark: hand-tooled and still unsold, by then four decades ancient, an icon crackling into dried mosaics shedding dust.

The gaming wheel was in the corner, its odd numbers painted black and its even numbers painted white. Tiny blades separated all one hundred numbers and silvered the circumference. A red felt tongue, smooth as the French percale on my grandparents' bed, lolled at the top when the wheel was at rest.

Without a word, we cousins lined up underneath it. This was Rosh Hashanah, the beginning of the Days of Awe. But, as always, we would open with a round of rock, paper, match or scissors. Because the stakes were high—the winner got first spin at the wheel—we all stared up at the ceiling or stared down at the sawdust on the earthen floor. With feigned indifference, we fiddled with the tiny pearls on our white gloves or brushed invisible scuffs from our good shoes, all of us having learned as if by genetic inheritance the importance of the poker face in public.

But tip-offs could be gleaned by secret scrutiny. So, from the corner of my eye, I watched my sister readjust her belt, and by this sign I knew she wasn't sure if she should stick with scissors—she'd been losing with it lately—or try another opening. My bookish cousin Dickie (the only boy among us) frowned and squinted, as if prematurely fitting his features to the inevitable stethoscope. My oldest cousin, Kitty, was on a hot streak and she knew it—crowned the beauty of a local swim club that July, she tilted back her head and smiled, as if the dusty sunshine streaming through the single window was a spotlight manned by her admirers and aimed right for her. She would stick with rock, no question. Lynn and Barb, Aunt Elsie's girls, were wild cards; they never strategized.

I closed my eyes and tried to concentrate on what I knew. The odds in this weren't even (in fact were never even, never), but favored scissors and rock: scissors could cut paper or match, and rock had the might to smash match or scissors, while match could only ignite paper, which could merely cover rock. But I also knew that while the powers of paper and match seemed relatively limited, a gutsy win could come from either. If you really wanted something, it was necessary to think and plan. You didn't stand on a soapbox like a beatnik in Manhattan's Greenwich Village. You had to choose your stance, stick with it, and never whine or welsh once the winner was declared, no matter how great your disappointment at the outcome, no matter how many times I settled on the rock, no matter how many times someone else flashed paper and covered my fist.

While being youngest of our clan sometimes entitled me to special treatment from my sister and my parents, I knew better than to exploit that lucky break by whining or welshing in my grandparents' garage. I knew that it was possible for a person to forget many things, to make careless mistakes or even premeditated ones, yet somehow live to tell the story. You could never, for instance, know your Hebrew name, but one day, you could ask your rabbi and he, somehow, would know the answer. You could go to Israel any day the spirit moved you and be taken in, no questions asked. You could even stand in court and ask a judge to change your surname from Moskowitz to Martin, deluding yourself that you simply wanted to assure Dickie's chances of getting into medical school when the time came to apply, as had my Aunt Bernice and Uncle Heshie, just a year before.

I knew about hope and I knew about *hubris*. From personal experience, I knew that during recess at school you could lock yourself in the girls' room and practice the dark art of lacing your hand from your forehead to the middle of your chest back and forth across your shoulders, just to see how it felt, to cop with the tips of your fingers an extra iota of power of use, if not in this world, then in the one that millions of gentiles believed came hereafter: gentiles invisible in our part of Newark, but reputed to reside everywhere else in the world in vast numbers. You could cross yourself and you could live to tell the story, although you didn't deserve to. And when finally you were finished, your betraying fingers committing their sacrilege right above the silver Star of David at your neck, you would burst into tears of real penitence and yank the john handle again and again, as if to flush there the proof of your treachery. Even a transgression as serious as that could be forgiven.

But I also knew that when it came to children, you must name them only after someone who was dead, not someone living, just as—no matter what—you must be buried as a Jew. You couldn't betray your people and choose to finally rest with strangers.

And I knew this too: no one would play with a person who had welshed on a bet, just as no one with any self-respect would consider it. If you welshed, your name wouldn't be worth the birth certificate *or* the judge's decree that it was stamped on. You'd be ruined.

Rock (the fist remained clenched), paper (a spread palm), scissors (two fingers spread), match (a single finger).

On the count of three, six arms flew into the center of our circle.

Their five hands splayed wide as paper. Alone, I took the long shot and gambled on a single finger.

Match.

And for the first time in my life, I won the opening spin.

So I lifted my hand to the gaming wheel's fine, solid curve as the year 5921, alias 1961, began.

That was the year we stopped renting on Schluy Street and bought our first house, on Keer Avenue. Schluy Street was only five minutes from my grandparents' house on Renner, but my parents and sister and I hadn't slept in Newark the night before. Because everything we owned was bundled for the movers, we had driven down the shore, to Bradley Beach. In the afternoon, riding the waves in my rubber safety tire, I had looked back at the sand and been astonished at the empty space between our blanket and the next.   That luxury never happened when we spent our annual two weeks down the shore with the rest of the family. During the season, a few inches between blankets signaled a day doomed to rain, and to make our shared turf seem grander, every part of the beach was known for something special: the teenagers crammed along the first block off Ocean Avenue; the families with children along the second; and along the third, the dark and handsome Sephardics from as far away as Brooklyn, gabbing in a foreign language not Yiddish and forbidden to my cousin Kitty for dating because of their strangeness. Still, those

Sephardics also were Jewish, and so they too had trekked to Bradley Beach. If another town down the shore was open to all of us then, no one we knew was aware of it.

That evening, with her suntanned arm linked through my father's, my mother had seemed a princess with her prince on royal holiday, in a sea-green skirt and halter top, and on her hand a new gold ring centered by an opal and two diamonds. She stopped to curl her palms against the rail along the boardwalk, and in the dusk, the opal sparkled blue and orange, a small but potent burst of fire. I dangled at the edge as she leaned forward. Bustling gulls were scavenging on the sand. My mother smiled, as if she knew them well and found unremarkable the way they pushed and shoved each other.

"You shouldn't have spent so much money," she told my father. "My sisters will spot it like *that*. You of all people should know that I wasn't raised to wear my money on my back."

He lifted a thick cigar from his pocket, struck a match against the railing and sucked until the end had caught the flame. The smoke masked his face, then drifted across the sand, out toward the waves.

"A little something worked out nicely with a supermarket king up in the Palisades last week. Better than even Nat expected," he said. "Magnificent place at the foot of the George Washington Bridge, with the skyline right there for the looking and all night long, great platters of lox and cold sliced filet. Of course, I got Nat the best liquor: Jack Daniels and Chivas and so forth. This guy couldn't lose his money fast enough," my father added. "In all my years with your brother, I've never seen anything like it."

"You mean, Nat couldn't take his money fast enough," said my mother.

He glanced our way, but my sister had wandered ahead and I'd decided to hang straight down, my sandals hooked onto the edge of the railing. It took my eyes several seconds to adjust to the dark beneath the boardwalk. Scattered pairs of teenagers were necking in the shadows of the splintered pilings. Sweaty shirts were riding up on untanned flesh and the tangles of arms and legs had slid into tender knots.

I tried to imagine the teenagers grown up and married, taking time from their slithering embraces to speak. I couldn't see it.

My parents' voices floated toward me, disembodied.

"Don't worry about the price. That ring fell off a truck. Do you

43

like it? The jeweler told me it was flawless."

"Peskin? He probably drove the truck. I love the ring."

My father lowered his voice, but between the smacks of white-caps, I could hear him. The gritty Romeos and Juliets were locked tight now, impossible to differentiate.

"What really gets me," he whispered, "is how some people work so hard to legitimately earn money, only to piss it away as if they'd gotten it for free. As long as I live, I'll never understand it."

Underneath the boardwalk, one of the boys lifted his hand from his girlfriend's neck and waved at me lethargically. That made me fall from the railing onto the beach.

"Are you okay?" my parents called. Further down the boardwalk, my sister crossed her arms and stared up at the first few stars, pre-tending she didn't know me.

My face and hands were full of sand. I ran along the beach and at the next stairs came back up onto the boardwalk. By then, we had crossed through Bradley and entered somber Ocean Grove, known to us as "Ocean Grave." Only with my father there did my sister and I ever dare take that invisible but dangerous border. Jewish chil-dren occasionally had been roughed up in Ocean Grave when they walked through to the games and rides at Asbury Park. Now we both strode bravely, lifting the silver Stars of David at our collars to make sure that they were hanging freely, for all the world to see.

And at the end of the boardwalk, Asbury Park roared up in rain-bow neon, just as Oz had burst into color when Dorothy emerged from her gray Kansas twister. The pungent smell of chlorine from the public bath house trysted with the salty evening air as scores of concession stands magically appeared: salt water taffy in rainbow colors, silver vats of cotton candy, hand-cut crinkled French fries in striped paper cones. Hucksters in red shirts waved soft-eyed stuffed giraffes and panda bears at the strolling crowd, thinner than in August but large enough to keep the effort worth their while.

By then, my sister had joined me. My mother was smiling and my father was laughing as he reached into the pocket of his Bermudas. In his short-sleeved white shirt and leather sandals, he looked as pure and cheerful as the Good Humor man who drove his truck around the rooming houses every afternoon at four o'clock in sea-son. All sorts of gifts from his suppliers tumbled out with his hand: a pen set from Seagram's, a tiny address book stamped "Gallo," two monogrammed chains for his masses of keys, a small flashlight courtesy of Black & White—my father loved all gadgets and gimmicks and, like my mother, anything free. He licked his thumb and flicked his finger at the rubber band encircling his thick wad of cash. In one graceful movement, the rubber band unfurled and zoomed down to bracelet his wrist. My father's fingers whirled through that mass of bills so skillfully I held my breath at the natural wonder of it, the sheer magnificence. But my father, who had been orphaned as a child, remained blasé. Having a family, intact and thriving, still struck him as the only form of wealth that he might not entirely deserve.

Usually my sister and I shared a five, but that night he peeled off two tens. He reached back in his pocket, jiggled the coins there, and came up with a fistful of shiny silver dollars.

The tens were crisp, their corners sharp. The slogan on the silver gleamed: *IN GOD WE TRUST*.

"Happy New Year, girls," my father said.

"Don't spend it all in one place," my mother cautioned. "Your father worked hard for that money."

On the Days of Awe, the colors of the grown-ups' clothes were always neutral, like the arid Newark landscape. The women wore navy or beige jacketed dresses, usually silks or lightweight knits, sometimes with a daring fleck in the fabric. Despite the heat, my grandmother insisted on carrying the mink stole my uncle had bought her. The men's suits invariably were black or gray. No matter how early the holidays might fall, no matter how steamy the weather, at Labor Day every vestige of white clothing except for fathers' shirts had gone into mothballs and cedar, not to be resurrected until Memorial Day. Such was fashion's first commandment. Not once did I see a Newarker of any creed break it.

On Bergen Street, all the stores used to close for the holidays. Posters at the Park Theater advertised Cecil B. DeMille's latest spectacle, but the marquee was specially lettered to wish us Happy New Year. Metal grates were rolled down on the lithe, long-legged mannequins in Miss Vivian's Belles Modes Shoppe; on the gleaming cases of Kosher beef and fresh-killed poultry hanging from metal hooks inside Dumbroff's; on the sapphires and diamonds at Peskin's; even, out of respect to its clientele and plain business sense, on the dusty plate-glass window of Kearney's hardware store.

In a few blocks, we neared the massive Catholic orphanage set back from the street and surrounded by a chain-link fence. The setting seemed appropriate, as if the only Christian outpost that could operate among us would have to do so without benefit of family or friends. The orphanage was named for a saint and never failed to get a reaction from the men, who considered the idea of anyone acting saintly every minute of his life a sweet but dangerous delusion. "Maybe when the real Messiah arrives, people will be perfect," laughed Uncle Nat as we passed the children playing in the scruffy yard, with no one but stone statues of Jesus and Mary to watch over them. "Not until then."

At the next intersection, shirtless workers were repaving the street, their sweat pooling in the hollows of their shoulder blades. The air smelled of molten tar, something like bubble gum, magnified a thousandfold. Early in the season, this pungency had signified a kind of rebirth, a sign of faith and democratic fairness from the big-shot *goniffs*, the elected thieves at City Hall, that our streets were as worthy of the tax dollar as any Newark neighborhood's. But by Rosh Hashanah, the smell had lost its metaphoric power and added too much heaviness to the air. We were nowhere near the smooth, new tar, but the men who were working on it stopped to stare uncomprehendingly at us as we passed—on a workday in America, none of our men were working. Who knew what crazy thing a Jew could do, from spite or just from mystifying differentness? We might suddenly turn *meshugina*, completely insane, and run from the sidewalk to ruin the wet tar, never mind the effect on our own shoes and streets.

By the time we turned up Chancellor Avenue's steep incline, our discomfort was acute. Lead weights seemed to bog our veins and our lips had grown too logy to form words. The steamy, breathless heat was another obstacle to overcome, one more strenuous day to tack on to the ancient forty in the Sinai and all the tough days that had followed. Splotches of perspiration appeared on the men's foreheads and on the backs of the women's dresses, spreading between their shoulders across the fabrics of their finest clothes. By these signs, I knew that never again would I jump in mountains of crisp fallen leaves, or ice-skate on the slickened pond in Weequahic Park, or watch spring's first robins and buds. We were trapped in endless summer. "Will you take a look at that sun," my father said.

Low against the river, it loomed like a giant tomato, the color of Jersey beefsteaks frying in oil. Past Frelinghuysen Avenue, the paths and fields of Weequahic Park were brown and silent. As if forced at gun point, green had fled our city and left it ashed in tan.

"Killer heat," my mother said.

"Forget Jerusalem," said Uncle Nat. "Let's pray for Montreal."

But my grandfather, alone among us, didn't seem to feel the heat at all. By now, Beth David's stone dome was visible in the distance and he strode briskly toward it. At a plain three-family house, the rest of us paused for breath and watched him go. Heat waves rose from the concrete, clouding his image; then he vanished altogether.

Long faded fingers of paint peeled down the doorway of the house where we had paused, along the porch, at the cock-eyed window frames.

"Look at that," said Uncle Nat. "Would you believe me if I told you that's the house where Longie Zwillman grew up? That's where he got his start."

In a patch of crabgrass, someone had planted a rock-bordered oval with geraniums, the petals bleached white now and curled into tiny hard lumps. A rusting tricycle lay on its side near the curb. One of the wheels was missing and the other two were flat.

"Longie Zwillman was a murderer, wasn't he?"

My cousin Dickie reported this as if it were a fact he had looked up in the encyclopedia at the Newark Public Library. "A big-time crook," he added.

My father pulled a pair of cigars from his breast pocket, crumpled the cellophane of one, and twirled the trunk between two fingers. He handed Nat the other cigar and one of my aunts' husbands quickly moved to light it for him. My grandmother yanked Dickie's collar and said something fast in Yiddish to my Aunt Bernice. "Hey," my cousin said. "I'm choking."

Bernice swiveled the toe of her high-heel against the sidewalk and stared in the opposite direction. "Too much TV," she shrugged.

"She's right, Nat," said Dickie's father. "The kids today watch far too much TV."

My father leaned down to cup my face inside his palm. "I hear you won first spin this morning."

"I did, Pop. I did."

"You're a helluva girl."

"I always thought Longie grew up in Elizabeth," Dickie's father was saying.

"'Longie'?" Nat said. "You know him personally?"

Dickie's father cleared his throat. "Longie Zwillman."

My father took my hand and smoothed out the fingers. He slipped onto my thumb the cigar's embossed paper ring, a tiny gold crown. My mother clucked in our direction and he said, "Sorry. *Heck* of a girl." Then he added, "Longie was born right here in Newark."

My mother pulled a Pall Mall from the pack she always carried, lit it and inhaled. She picked a few bits of tobacco from her lips and stood there, one elbow cupped in the palm of her other hand. "A local hero," she said. "A fine New Jersey boy."

"Like Woodrow Wilson," my sister said. "Like Grover Cleveland."

Aunt Elsie squinted at my mother's hair. "You know, it looks a little lighter. I didn't notice it before, but now I do. You're not bleaching it, are you, Lillian?"

My mother's face went blank, as it often did when the family gathered together. She tossed the cigarette on the sidewalk and with the toe of her high heel, rubbed it into nothingness. "I'm not bleaching it," she said.

Elsie shrugged. "It looks a little lighter. I thought maybe you were having it done."

Aunt Bernice still was marveling about the shabby house in front of us. "Look how small. I bet that whole place is the size of one room in the house that Zwillman lives in now."

"Longie? You know it is," laughed Nat.

The static air blued with rich cigar smoke, the plume of men and far-off autumn. On Chancellor Avenue a police car inched along, sunlight glinting from the fender. "That cop is a straight arrow," said my father, waving. "One of the few I've ever met. When his kids were small, he always accepted a little something around Christmas. But now they're grown, and the poor dumb guy takes nothing."

"Longie Zwillman was a man who worked very hard and made it big," my grandmother told us. "He started in concessions, like your uncle. But he's no one you children ever will run into. You'll go to college, be someone. You'll make us proud."

My sister turned to my mother. "Meyer Lansky's house in Florida was tiny too," she told her. "Remember?"

My mother frowned and bent to retie the bow around my sister's waist. "No. I don't."

But we all had seen that stucco bungalow the year before, during Christmas break from school. We were staying for two weeks at the house that Nat had bought my grandparents in Miami Beach; my father came down to join us for the last four days. One night, he tried to drive us to an ice cream shop near Lincoln Road, but he lost his way. He turned down a lane of modest houses with jalousied windows and an occasional royal palm out front. "Where the hell am I?" he asked my mother. "Are we still in Florida?"

When she glanced up and read aloud the sign, his tan seemed to fade all at once.

"My God," he told her. "You know who owns here?"

He pulled to the strip of grass separating two of the bungalows. In the yard on the right, I could see a small plastic wading pool, the kind even babies can't drown in. Part of the pool was taped with Band-Aids. A blue bottle of seltzer and an orange box of dog biscuits sat on the grass beside an old man aslant on a plastic chaise *lounge*, rubbing his legs with an ooze of red gel.

Meyer Lansky dipped his feet into the wading pool and whistled. A fat dachshund came bursting from a neighbor's yard. Lansky reached into the orange box and fed the dog a biscuit.

"That's the place," my father had whispered. "That's him. Nat was over here."

My mother leaned over, squinting out his open window. "I don't see any bodyguards."

"Lansky's another case entirely," my father said. "Dresses simply, lives plain, no frills. They say that, for him, it's strictly the intellectual challenge. Like a calling. Like any professional. But an oddball. Definitely an oddball."

In the women's balcony of Beth David, a rusted fan whirled noisily, scalping blades of heat across us. Someone had propped open the front doors of the *shul* and the windows were raised, but the air stayed in place, so soupy that most of the women were using their programs to fan their faces as they prayed for a powerful breeze. The metal of the folding chair made me jump when the backs of my knees touched the seat. My perspiration kept sliding me down into the narrow space before the next row of chairs. "Rabbi Kessler just opened the altar," my sister reported as everyone stood. "He lifted the Torah into his arms and is heading through the men. Gramp is reaching out to kiss it with his fingers."

The fan in the corner sputtered and failed. The women lurched forward, straining and jostling, a vast perfumed surge toward the sacred scrolls that were making their way down the aisle beneath us. Instinctively, I moved my lucky hand to my heart, forgetting, for a moment, that we were not in school, that Rabbi Kessler was not my teacher, commanding us to civic piety through recitation of the Pledge of Allegiance. All around me earrings dangled, zippers glinted, nylon stockings gathered sun. The hard oblong atolls of hidden garters strained between flesh and damp fabric. A thick stripe as light as sky-writing shot down the leg of the aunt standing in front of me, widening to a cloudy fret above her nylon-covered heel.

My grandmother leaned forward to speak to me. "Why don't you go down to the railing, my *kinder*? You'll have a better view from there."

I bent my head and made my way among the women, waving my program at my sticky face and neck. My grandmother reached in her purse and unwrapped a small square packet.

"Don't fan yourself," she counseled, handing me a Wash-'n'-Dri. "You use up more energy that way and get hotter. You waste away your strength. And once you waste your strength, anything can happen. When you get to the edge, stand still and think cool. Think of being down the shore, swimming in the ocean."

Our block of seats was only six rows up the balcony, but with each step down, the air seemed less oppressive. At the railing, I lifted the Wash-'n'-Dri to my forehead; the alcohol stung my sunburned skin. On Friday evenings down the shore in August, when the men left their work in Newark to join us for the weekend, I would lean over the railing of our rooming house in just this way, peering past the chains of women chatting on the porches as they rocked in metal chairs the shape of sea-shells, and I would picture a long, virile caravan of Conestoga wagons braving any humid hardship to make their way to us. In my mind, the same men who might be stopped at stands along the highway were blazing through cactuses clumped beside scruffy brush and sifting for gold in fast-moving, dangerous rivers. When night fell, they sat around campfires whose flames shot to the sky and told the stories that sustained them—stories of beloved wives and children—while yearning bachelors like Nat wiped the powder from their smoking guns, entranced by the luck of their partners in having such ties.

Sometimes, when there was no game to kill and no water for miles, the men's hunger and thirst made them see visions whose precise shape and texture I could only imagine as a circular steel-gray whirl. But whatever the men had seen, whatever it was they had felt, gave them the strength to overcome any obstacle and keep moving toward us.

At the railing of Beth David's balcony, my Wash-'n'-Dri had shriveled to a tough towelette. My father's cigar ring still smelled faintly of tobacco, but its embossed ridges were flat with humidity when I finally spotted him standing at the start of our men, his big head bowed slightly. He was fiddling with the grosgrain ribbon in the middle of his prayer book, tapping his foot to some secret rhythm. His lips were pursed—I thought he might actually be whistling. Later this evening, when the sun had set, he would change from his good suit back into work clothes and drive to the Central Ward, just to make sure everything at his tavern was as it should be. Not until Yom Kippur would we see him in a suit again, unless Nat called to ask for help with his concessions.

After my father came Heshie and Lou, the lesser uncles-by-marriage. Then my cousin Dickie. Then my grandfather, Jacob Edelman, born Yakov and a surname that I couldn't pronounce. He stood in place among the others, but he was *davening* passionately from the waist, his fingers entwined in the fringes of his silky prayer shawl. His eyes were now open, now closed, aimed at his prayer book, then up at the Torah as he rocked back and forth. But his mouth was moving quickly in a private murmur to his God; sociability was not his goal. I wondered if he even realized that he was in a crowded sanctuary, or if all the weekday mornings and the Friday evenings when he walked alone here had inured him to the swell of others now, on Rosh Hashanah. A *mensch*, my grandmother called him. A human being. Head in the clouds, hands on the Talmud. But, she always added, a man who never had it in him to charge enough or to collect what was his.

He kept *davening*, his eyes tightly shut now. I looked and wondered: which were the pictures that moved in private beneath those thin lids, blue-veined like road maps? Which distant landmarks still burned bright in his heart, forty years later and thousands of miles from the place of his birth? Did he still hear and smell the gathering swell of ancient blood-lust? At the aisle on the main floor of the sanctuary, his grown son stood beside him, silent and unmoving as a statue made of steel.

Nat was the tallest of our men, fine-featured and nearly as dark as a Sephardic. He stood with his hands clasped behind his back and his legs apart, as if he were perpetually at ease. Sunlight glinted off his manicured fingernails. At twenty-one, Nat had voted for Franklin Roosevelt's final term. After that, he voted for Harry Truman and Dwight Eisenhower. If John Kennedy ran for president in the next election, Nat planned to vote for him. "No one can stomach a loser," he always told us. In August, down at Bradley, we cousins would encircle him while he shuffled playing cards into spires and bridges with such graceful ease it seemed as if spades and diamonds floated in the salty air. Aces converted into deuces right before our eyes; kings and queens flew above the sand and landed in my mother's bag of fruit. We picked a card, any card, and slid it back inside the deck. Anyone who chose could cut the deck and *still* Nat eased the card out at first try. Without troubling to glance down, he could tell which card it was. With little urging, he repeated any trick that we demanded, in slow motion if we wanted. "That's not something I ordinarily agree to do," he often said. "But of course you kids are blood."

Act Two was the dice: several pairs of white and a few that flashed translucent red, also a single pair that was bright green. But no matter how many times we guessed eight, seven came up. And no matter how many times we guessed five, eleven came up. And if we guessed three, it was two, and if we guessed twelve, it was ten. So then big-shot Dickie had to roll the dice himself, juggling a pair and breathing at his palms, as he had seen our uncle do, before letting go of them.

But unless Nat rolled, the numbers always came up wrong.

I leaned further over the railing, straining for a better view, to study from a distance those familiar faces. Now that I had found them, my father and my uncles seemed always to have been where

I had looked just moments earlier. The men in my family were a sober and dignified group, today as at all times discreet and well-mannered. They stood respectfully now, of course, but also whenever a woman entered the room, even if the room was my grandparents' kitchen and the woman was one of my aunts. Unlike my grandfather, my father and uncles shaved every day, sometimes twice daily, and the creamy skin on their faces smelled wonderfully—my father's of Old Spice, Nat's of French cologne. Their teeth were white as my grandfather's beard and I had never heard any of them raise his voice.

My father often said this calmness was crucial: that for anyone involved in concessions, it was necessary to think and plan. The night before at Asbury Park, he had stood on the boardwalk while I dangled below, and he told my mother about men like the supermarket king up in the Palisades, who abandoned themselves to the worship of luck. That kind of idolatry gave off a smell, a stench that made a working man, even one who knew the score, reel from the shock of unabashed waste: on the way to the john, my father had seen Persian rugs in the *kids'* bedrooms. "I an talking," he told my mother, "about expensive ancient patterns littered with the broken toys of children." His voice had gotten low and level then, the way it did when he was baffled at stupidity. This supermarket king up in the Palisades went too far for a working man who knew the value of a dollar. The king had a game room in his house. A *game room*. He pissed away his good fortune on a separate room for self-indulgence, when anyone raised on the streets, anyone with eyes in his head, anyone like my father could have told him: *If you've learned anything at all in your lucky years on this earth, then get out of this game. Right now. Just walk away.*

From my watch at the balcony railing, none of our men looked anything like the way I imagined that supermarket king, or the red-faced yodeling hucksters at the concessions on the boardwalk down at Asbury Park, or like my father did from time to time when he left us late at night and went to help Nat with *his* concessions. I couldn't detect any resemblance at all.

But they didn't look much like my grandfather, either. All those men standing side by side, my men, were a single image out of focus, a wavering mirage in which the eyeballs roam from their sockets and each of the hands appears to have ten fingers instead of five and the skin does not fit the bones.

I wondered how I would ever resolve that blur of white shirts and black suits, those mismatched hearts and minds, of my own flesh and blood.

At that moment, a feather of blue appeared in the lumpish sky above Chancellor Avenue. At the altar, Rabbi Kessler lifted his arm and the long, hopeful sob of the *shofar* rang out: that low, visceral sound, a ram's-horn trumpet opening into the past and the future, carved from bone of animal by tribes of sandy Israelites roaming on an ancient desert without an ocean to imagine, let alone a homeland of their own.

Then the blue elongated, striating the brownish haze of sky and tautening into cobalt, wisped with white like strands of cotton candy. From the opened doors and windows, a cooling breeze sailed toward us. The women laughed like girls as the hems of their new dresses flicked their stockinged legs. The men grappled with the *yarmulkes* fluttering on their skulls, grinning in the face of this gutsy proof that, any time and without warning, something stronger than another man could come along to make its power known.

Remembered, acknowledged, secure in community, we opened our mouths. The *shofar* blew again and our most plaintive prayer began.

Sh'ma Yisroel, Adonai Elohenu. The Lord is Our God, The Lord is One.

The breeze became a wind. The months of cramped heat bellowed into vastness. The leaves on the trees along Chancellor Avenue lifted themselves up and snapped to attention with seasonal fire, as if God Himself had tired of feigning pluralistic allegiance to January 1, a day that never varied from the one before or after: if the sky heaved snow on December 31, it would snow again the next day. Overhead, an airplane roared from Newark Airport, punctual to the crest of voices chanting the *Sh'ma.* Downstairs on the main floor of the sanctuary, the tip of my grandfather's beard brushed his opened prayer book. His creased, shadowed face looked painted in oils.

Standing open-mouthed among my people, I could hear myself breathe and feel my heart beat: like lifting my hand to the wheel on

Renner Avenue, gripped by the numbers blurring to union, while my confusing blood pumped through every vein and artery—as if, at my creation, He had cupped my burning flesh within His palms, bent to press His lips against the varied parts comprising me, then tossed me down upon this swirling earth to see what, between the two of us, could possibly result.

MARCH OF DIMES

To hear Miss Powderly tell the story, the human heart presided deep within our chests and sent out diligent prophets, which she termed pulses, to outlying areas needing a boost. These pulses commandeered the surface of the skin, beating out their singular message. You could feel proof of these prophets in the most forlorn places—for instance, in the fleshy parts of your wrists and on the bones at the sides of your face, which Miss Powderly ecumenically called "temples" rather than churches. Lesser pulses crooned their gentle sermonettes at the throat, forehead, even on the thin skin of your ankles.

All that week, Miss Powderly stood at her blackboard reciting her litany: "that the heart was neither red nor heart-shaped, and had no cleft between curves, no point at the bottom." She told us to clench our fists and hold them up. She claimed our hearts were shaped like that, but damp and slithery, more grayish-blue than red in color. None of us believed her, but no one said a word.

What I remember best about Miss Powderly is her punctuality, how the gestures of her hands seemed so finely timed to her expressions, and the way that these combined to reveal her attitude about us. We knew her very well, having observed her day after day after day, and especially in those early minutes of the morning, when the rules required that we look straight at her while she led us in reciting her Lord's Prayer, same as every teacher in our school did every morning. While she said those words aloud, we were supposed to clasp our hands and recite along. But most of us mumbled or didn't speak at all, although of course we knew the prayer by heart. We couldn't help but know it. We'd been hearing it day after day ever since kindergarten.

Miss Powderly loved the prayer. She thought the words were beautiful. To her, saying those words couldn't hurt a soul. "Why you won't say them escapes me," she told us, like clockwork, each morning.

When she finished the Lord's Prayer, Miss Powderly always sighed, as though she regretted the start of the day's secular subjects. With a down-turned mouth she gazed at the ceiling, as if somebody up there was giving her private instructions on what to do next. Had I been a different sort of child, I might have looked in my heart and found compassion for her: after years and years of teaching in our part of Newark, she still couldn't figure us out. Always, Miss Powderly required a few moments to remember her secular mission. So, in silence, we gazed out the window and waited.

Out above the playground, a gang of pigeons twittered on the telephone wires. The sixth-graders, who started school fifteen minutes after us, were gathering near the steps. My sister and her friend Paula Eisenberg stood talking with some other girls. At the hoops, the Salzman twins were dribbling two basketballs, trying to impress all the girls. The best shooter in the school was a boy named Mark Shumofsky but he wasn't out there, so after a while the twins lost interest and hurled the balls against the wire fence. A strong breeze blew across the playground and my sister grabbed the hem of her poodle skirt to hold it down while Paula, who was starting to develop, clutched her arms across her chest, as if the breeze might blow away her tiny breasts.

The thirty desks in my class were pushed together in boy-girl pairs and I shared mine with Larry Eisenberg, Paula's brother. Across the aisle from us, Ivan Plotnik had been tickling Amy Siegel's neck. He stopped and motioned Larry over. Larry leaned into the aisle and the two boys' foreheads touched.

Ivan said, "Your sister's got nice knockers."

Larry cupped his hands and pumped them up and down, as though he were a butcher, measuring out two slabs of brisket. "Yep, Paula's off to a good start."

At the front of the room, Miss Powderly was clapping her hands to make an announcement.

"The bus that the fifth-graders rented for their trip to the Statue of Liberty is too big for them."

We were all glad to hear it.

"Whoever brings a permission slip and five dollars to school to-morrow can visit the Statue. Have your mothers pack a lunch," she told us. "And wear warm clothing. There's a park where we can picnic."

A little while later, she went to the supply closet and took out the week's collection canisters for the March of Dimes campaign. The class that collected the most in New Jersey got a visit to Trenton to meet the governor.

"Until there's a cure for polio I want you to remember some-thing," Miss Powderly said as she passed out the canisters. "If you must use the bathroom tomorrow at the Statue, then make sure to cover the seat in several layers of toilet paper. And squat—don't touch. You don't want to pick up any germs."

The boys guffawed at this remark and the girls pretended that they hadn't heard. The instant Miss Powderly turned her back, a few spitballs flew across the room and landed on top of the gerbils' cage. Just then, Larry leaned toward me. He smelled faintly of his breakfast, which always was oatmeal with cinnamon, and more viv-idly of the forbidden stick of chewing gum wadded in his cheek.

"Boys don't squat, ha-ha-ha."

At the blackboard, Miss Powderly stood rapping her pointer to get our attention. Behind us in their wire cage, the gerbils gnawed on their breakfast pellets.

"There will be all sorts of people at the Statue," our teacher told us. "There will be colored people."

When she lifted the chalk to start on arithmetic, Miss Powderly's whole body seemed to shudder, as if her own heart had skipped a beat or two, just thinking about the dangers awaiting us the next day on Liberty Island.

Later that afternoon, Larry and I were coming out of Pollack's Delicatessen, where I had bought a bag of french fries and pig Larry as usual had bought two bags, along with a large sour pickle.

"Toilet seats," I scoffed. "That's not how you get polio."

Larry swallowed his last fry, crumpled up his second empty bag and reached for some of mine. "I know how you get it."

Although Larry said this as a statement, I knew he meant it as a question. In fact, the less sure Larry was of something, the more certain he always seemed about it. But because I didn't respond, he walked too close to me along the sidewalk and licked his salty fingers in as disgusting a manner as possible. Then he ran a few feet ahead, turned around so I'd be sure to see him, and did awful things with the pickle, trying to make my face grow red. Which Larry didn't realize was impossible, as no one in my family ever blushed. It wasn't in our blood, my grandmother said.

"You get polio from walking around in a wet bathing suit or swimming too soon after you eat," Larry told me. "That's why you have to wait an hour."

When I didn't answer he broke down, as I'd expected, and stopped pretending he knew everything. His voice trembled. "Isn't it?"

I pushed away his elbow and looked up the street toward the Beth Israel Hospital, high on the hill four blocks west, where Mark Shumofsky had been living since summer in an iron lung. Something had been wrong with the vaccine that his doctor used and now Mark was even worse off than my grandfather. Gramp had had a stroke that spring, and stayed six weeks in the hospital, but at least he could still move half of his body. With half his mouth, he still could speak. Mark Shumofsky couldn't move either of his legs or arms, he couldn't move his mouth at all or breathe without the Beth Israel's iron lung. He might never again shoot a basketball.

"Think what you want," I told Larry as I kicked a hill of leaves along the curb at The Bergen Bake Shoppe. The leaves were dry and brittle but I liked their bite against my legs, on the smooth skin below my skirt, above my socks. "It's a free country."

Larry grabbed a branch of the nearest oak tree and swung himself across the sidewalk. Mrs. Mittleman rapped the window with a metal spatula and waved her arms—*Be careful*, she was mouthing to him. Larry let go of the branch and pretended to crash onto the sidewalk as I kept walking. Behind me he repeated, as if I hadn't heard the first time, "Isn't that how you get polio?"

The thing that always amazed me about Larry was how one minute he could do something to make me feel like a nobody, and next minute ask my opinion about something important. The only way I could bridge that gap in Larry, the one between his pantomime with the pickle and the question about polio, was to pretend that he was actually two different boys trapped in one body. If I waited a while, the second boy could be someone worth answering.

When he caught up with me I said, "No one knows how you get polio. And anyone who pretends to know is just a liar."

"Well, I'm never getting paralyzed. Or you either." And as if to prove it to us both, Larry suddenly added, "Race you to the corner."

Because Mark Shumofsky had been one of his main heroes, I stayed where I was and considered letting Larry win. But at the last second, my muscles took over and we finished in a dead heat, as usual. While we panted for breath, the city bus rumbled toward us.

That afternoon, my mother was taking my sister to the orthodontist and I was going to my father's tavern in the Central Ward. So far, our class had done pretty well in the March of Dimes Campaign, but it was going to be tough to get the total higher. Between the kids our age and the older ones who collected for Israeli trees, our neighborhood had been licked nearly clean. On our last door-to-door effort, Larry and I barely had collected a dollar for the paralyzed children.

"You can come with me. We can go collecting at my father's," I told him.

Larry threw the rest of the pickle in the street, stuck his hands in his pockets, and squinted at the sky. Then he looked down, kicked a stone into the street and said, "I'd better call my mother."

"You can call from my father's." I pointed in the opposite direction, toward Grumman Avenue, where Bobby Goldman lived. "Unless you want to go over there right now and tell Bobby you give up."

Bobby Goldman was Larry's arch-enemy. He was in the other fourth-grade class and Larry wanted more than anything in the world for ours to beat his in the March of Dimes campaign, even if we never got near the governor. So he followed me onto the bus and we sat in my favorite place at the back, over the wheels, where our bodies would feel every pothole and bump.

Then, as now, Broad and Market Streets were the central arteries that formed Newark's heart. But in those days, in the thriving department stores that radiated from their healthy intersection—at ultra-fancy Hahne's and pleasant, well-stocked Bamberger's; at so-

so Ohrbach's and at bargain basement Klein's—people milled harmoniously, as if the city truly were a melting pot set to simmer and not to boil over. And at certain times throughout the year, all of Newark seemed a natural unity. On summer afternoons, when every inch of air felt like a bullet packed with heat; in winter, when a quilt of snow blanketed us equally; in spring, when the sky above was vast and clear and blue: on those days when the weather seemed the essence of whichever season we were in, it was easy to imagine that through the over-landscaped gardens of North Newark, past the twisted alleys of Down Neck, up to Vailsburg's dense two-family houses, across the congested Central Ward and back toward us in aspiring Weequahic, every Newarker inhaled and felt glad to be alive, or shivered from the cold, or sweated in discomfort, as if we truly were one civic body experiencing in a single, physical sensation.

Of course, our part of the city belonged to us, and the other parts belonged to other people. The separate neighborhoods never truly intersected, despite the illusion created down at Broad and Market. And yet, if Larry and I had been riding in a covered wagon guarded by the U.S. cavalry or in an armored truck headed for Fort Knox, I would have felt no safer than I felt on that city bus as it crossed Chancellor, Lyons, Clinton Avenue.

Beside me on the plastic seat, Larry was staring out the window, his eyes wide and, for once, his mouth shut, watching the buildings grow closer and closer together, and the white people grow fewer and fewer. "Wow," he finally whispered. "It's different here."

But I was thrilled to be moving further from our part of the city, where everyone was known. As the lawns grew smaller and smaller, then finally disappeared; as the synagogues became Catholic and Methodist and Baptist churches; as more and more of those we then called "Negroes" began to fill the streets, I began to feel as if Larry and I were on a voyage to somewhere exotic. Something had changed in the landscape, and now I was noticeable within it. I was standing out.

I was excited by all this. The self that had to swelter every Rosh Hashanah and Yom Kippur on a folding metal chair in the women's balcony of our synagogue, while the men enjoyed cool comfort on the first floor's wooden pews; the self who had to sit and listen to whatever crazy story Miss Powderly chose to tell us—to clench our fists and pretend the human heart was shaped as brutally as that;

and the self who had to tolerate the jokes about Paula Eisenberg's new breasts: those selves were slipping from me like false skins as our bus headed to the Central Ward, a place which, except for our own neighborhood, I knew more intimately than any part of Newark.

Sherman Carter waved at me from behind the curved oak bar when I led Larry into my father's tavern. Sherman was lean and muscular, with skin so dark and gleaming that, even indoors, he seemed to be in spotlight. My father liked to kid that Sherman buffed himself nightly and used a thick coat of shellac, so he could scare any white people he might happen to run into. Mostly the white people he ran into lived on our street, Keer Avenue. Whenever my father's car was in the shop to be repaired, Sherman drove him home. Often they'd get out and lean against the hood of Sherman's car, chatting as they puffed on thick cigars. The neighbors always rolled their eyes and muttered comments. But they didn't cause trouble.

No customers were at the tables in the tavern yet. Things wouldn't start "hopping," as my father always put it, until later when night fell. "Your people come out of the woodwork after dark, just like cock-a-roaches," he liked to tell Sherman. I never could tell if Sherman thought this was funny or not. "My people come out to pay *your* people," he said.

I showed Larry the wooden phone booth in the corner, and by the time I climbed up on one of the leather stools, Sherman had poured two tall glasses of seltzer and was mixing in the U-Bet Chocolate Syrup. He added a shot of milk to each and stirred it all up with a long spoon.

"Here you go, Sugar. You're right on time." He slid the glasses over and tapped two straws on the bar. When the sheaths of paper sidled down, he plunged the straws into our glasses. Nobody else drank egg creams at the tavern, not even Sherman's children, who came by more often since they lived just around the corner. His kids preferred root beer, which I thought tasted like soap suds. There was a big bottle of it on the shelf in the refrigerator, alongside the milk and U-Bet.

"Where's Pop?" I asked him.

"At the bank, counting his millions. He'll be back in a few minutes."

"Tomorrow my class is going to the Statue of Liberty," I told him. "We weren't supposed to, but there's room on the bus."

"It's always nice when that happens." Sherman leaned his elbows on the bar and winked toward the phone booth. He grinned and his teeth looked like Chiclets, all even and white. "Who's that handsome fellow yonder making eyes at you?"

I shuddered. "That's Larry Eisenberg. He's just a kid in my class."

"Ah," Sherman said. "What a relief. I thought you might be planning to marry him instead of me."

I had told him that once, when I was so small I thought I could marry whoever I wanted, and Sherman never let me forget it.

"You're married," I reminded him. "You have a wife. Anyway, I'm not marrying anyone. I'm going to college."

"You could go to college *and* get married. Lots of girls do."

"Well, I never met one," I told him, and spun around on my stool until Larry came out of the phone booth. He guzzled his egg cream, then asked Sherman for another.

"You'll get sick," I warned Larry. "The way that you eat."

But Sherman made him a second egg cream and Larry downed it. Then he asked for some pretzels and Sherman plucked a bag from the metal rack. He popped open the cellophane between his big hands, gave Larry the bag and started stacking the shelves with clean glassware, from a solid base of goblets to tall frosty tumblers and squat ones for drinks-on-the rocks, with the shot glasses, tiny as thimbles, balanced on top. When Sherman went out to meet a delivery truck, I took Larry to the back of the tavern. There was a pool table there, next to a gleaming chrome jukebox with red neon trim. Best of all was the pinball machine, top of the line, with double flippers and what seemed like hundreds of lights. In the late afternoons, before the customers came in, Sherman or my father always fixed it so I could keep playing with the same quarter.

In no time, I was beating Larry by several thousand points, which in pinball is really not as much as it sounds. Larry kept yanking the starting plunger in and out after the outcome was obvious; he wasn't thrilled to quit a loser. But since I played pinball more often than he did, my winning was only natural.

"Mark Shumofsky came here once with my sister," I told him, to pick up his spirits. "He beat me good."

"Mark came *here?* No kidding." Larry ran his hand over the machine, as if touching the same place his idol had touched might make him an expert at pinball, too. I handed him his collection can.

"Maybe Mark will get better," I said. "Franklin Delano Roosevelt had polio and he became a President. He traveled all over the world. And my grandfather can squeeze my hand hard, even though the doctors said he never would."

The front door banged open. Sherman returned with two men wheeling stacks of boxes on top of metal dollies. They set the boxes next to the juke box and Sherman signed a paper clipped to a board.

"FDR was a great president," Sherman nodded. "FDR was tough. He was a survivor."

The first man squinted at the clipboard where Sherman had signed my father's name. Sherman headed for the stockroom and the delivery men watched him without speaking. Finally, the taller one called out.

"Hey, buddy. Are you trying to tell me you're Victor Tarlow?"

Sherman turned and held both palms in the air, as if someone had pulled a gun and he figured that surrendering was smarter than struggling. At first, his face muscles didn't move. Then he grinned.

"Do I *look* like Vic Tarlow? I ask you. This here's his daughter, the real boss of the show. Even Vic takes his orders from this girl. She'll vouch for me."

Over the years, I had seen all sorts of things at the tavern. One time, two young men came in to chat with my father, then went to their car and returned with their arms full. "These fell off a truck," they said, and for hardly any money my father got a new adding machine and my sister got her first camera. Another time, my father shoved a stack of cash into a paper bag and handed it to a policeman, who walked next door and emerged with a second plump paper bag. But I'd never seen anyone question Sherman about anything.

I shrugged and held my collection can to the delivery men. They each slid in a quarter.

"Sherman nearly runs this place," I told them. "Just ask anybody."

As Larry and I walked out into the fresh air, I thought again about Miss Powderly, and the unattractive look of my pale clenched fist compared to the large beauty of a real, pointed red heart, and her wild claim that pulses beat behind the knees of all human beings. There were no pulses in my grandfather's knees the day I checked there, or beneath his temples either, and I thought maybe I would report her for bad teaching when Larry and I met the governor.

"Do you think that there are germs in outer space? Do you ever think maybe it'll be the Russians who find the cure, and then they won't let us have it? Or the Red Chinese?"

Larry's lips still were smeared with egg cream as we headed to Kaminsky's Corner Mart. Normally he didn't think about big questions, he just listened to whatever anybody told us, and then he always argued when I came up with evidence that we'd been lied to. But that afternoon, he was rambling non-stop. Except for the owners of the stores in the Central Ward, everyone we saw was Negro.

"We're going to find the cure first, don't worry," I told him. "Then we're going to give it to the Russians, and when their paralyzed kids start walking again they'll remember, and that will be the end of war. We'll give it to all those other countries too." At school, we had spent the afternoon discussing life behind the many nations of the Iron Curtain. "Poland. Romania. Hungary. We'll give it to all of them."

At the next store the owner, Mr. Horowitz, folded up a pair of dollar bills and slid one each into the slots of our cans. But Larry's mind was elsewhere.

"What about East Germany?" he said when we came out.

I hesitated. Miss Powderly had talked a lot about East Germany. President Kennedy had gone there and told the world that he, too, was a Berliner. Miss Powderly said that we should cheer him on, no questions asked: no matter where our grandparents came from, or why they were no longer there, we should all believe the same now.

"I'm not sure about the East Germans," I told Larry. "Or about the West Germans, either."

At the local butcher's, we hit gold. When Sherman's cousin Pollard, who worked behind the counter, rang open the register and gave us every one of the coins in it, Larry was amazed. But he was even more astounded by the gleaming showcases stocked with raw pork ribs, slabs of bacon, and the spongy off-white grids of tripe so beloved in the Central Ward. At the corner mart, Mr. Kaminsky produced two fifty-cent pieces and a Chunky for Larry, then disappeared into the back of his store to go over his account books. The fifty-cent pieces didn't fit in the slots of the collection cans, so we tucked them into our socks. "I need some air," Larry said as he stood up. "I don't feel so good. I think I'll wait outside."

In the corner of the store, an older boy in sneakers and a Central High School sweatshirt was carrying cereal boxes up a ladder propped against the shelves. I went over and raised my collection can to his feet.

"Can you give us something for the March of Dimes campaign?"

He set his last carton on the top shelf and walked backwards down the ladder.

"Sure I can," he said, and ran the tip of his index finger underneath my neck. His skin was dark as Sherman Carter's, his touch was cool and firm, his mouth so near to mine as he leaned into my face that, if I had stuck out my tongue, its tip might have brushed his lips. Of course I didn't blush, but I could feel the goose-bumps as his finger came to rest on the first button of my coat.

I would outrun any danger, I would out-distance disaster. All afternoon, my whole body had felt wonderful, skipping for entire blocks without tripping once, or hopping on one foot and then the other without hitting a single crack in the sidewalk, while the coins in our collection cans got heavier and heavier and made a lively sound jumping up against the sides. Yet now, for the longest moment, I stood alongside the ladder in Mr. Kaminsky's Corner Mart, unable to move forward, backward, up, down, in any direction at all.

Then the boy dropped a coin into my canister and started to laugh—from malice or confusion, I never knew—he laughed as I ran for freedom.

Larry had been watching the whole time through the window. "We ought to tell your father about that kid," he smirked when I came out.

Once, when my parents had taken my sister and me to Radio City Music Hall in New York City, a man sitting behind us leaned over and breathed on my sister's neck. My father chased him through the audience and out into the lobby, where two security guards pulled him off and took the other man away. I knew if I said one word to my father about the boy in Mr. Kaminsky's store, that boy wouldn't be able to run far enough. He might as well run straight to the emergency room at St. Michael's Hospital, because that's where he'd wind up.

"Mind your own bees-wax," I told Larry. "That kid gave me a quarter, so there."

By then, the sunlight had started to vanish. Shadows began to appear. More and more people were stepping from the city buses and filling the streets. None of the men looked as if they'd touch me. But just to be safe, I approached only women.

Everybody knew about polio, no matter who they were or where they lived, everybody had read about Mark Shumofsky in the *Newark News* and was afraid. By the time the sun had set, both of our collection cans were full. As Larry and I shook them, we couldn't hear a thing.

When we got back to my father's tavern, my mother was sitting on a stool at the bar with her legs crossed, smoking a Pall Mall and sipping a glass of hot tea. Sherman and my father were checking the shelves to make sure there was enough of everything needed for the night. A few early-bird customers chatted at a corner table, drinking beers.

The jukebox was on and an old guy was crooning. My mother's eyes were half-closed as she tapped her fingers on the bar. She looked like she thought the old guy was singing special for her. "That Frank's got some set of pipes," she said.

"For a white boy," said Sherman, and everyone laughed.

My mother waved at me and Larry, turned back to Sherman and made a little face. "Frank's the best," she told him. "You've got to admit it."

I went over to my sister, who was leaning against one of the pinball machines, fiddling with the readjusted wires in her teeth.

"Look how great we did," I told her. "We filled both cans. Plus, this."

I pulled the fifty-cent piece from my sock and held it up. Larry bent to get his, but groaned as he leaned forward. By then, he barely could walk. His stomach was killing him from all the junk he had eaten.

"Oooh," he said, and sat down at a table.

My mother went over and put her palm on his forehead as Sherman walked out from the bar to go into the bathroom. "You don't have a fever," she told Larry.

"He's got a stomach ache," I said. "He had two egg salad sandwiches at lunch instead of one, like everybody else. He had a pack of gum and two bags of fries after school. Plus a pickle. Then he had two egg creams and a bag of pretzels. And a Chunky that Mr. Kaminsky gave him."

"I don't feel good," Larry said.

My mother smiled. "I bet you don't. You'd better use the bathroom before we leave."

Sherman was just coming out of it. The song on the jukebox had ended, and one of the early-birds was pushing more buttons. My sister was staring at the pirates and dancing girls painted on the pinball machine, the pirates in their blousey shirts and pantaloons and the dancing girls in nearly nothing. I wondered if she was thinking about Mark Shumofsky, and how normal and healthy he'd looked when he came here, hooting and hollering as he racked up more points. The truth was that Mark Shumofsky was the best pinball player I'd ever seen. He was a natural.

"We're going to the Statue of Liberty tomorrow," I told her.

"Hey, that's great. Our class went two years ago. A Jewish girl wrote a poem on a plaque there."

She picked the wine bottle-lamp from the table where Larry was holding his stomach and put it to her mouth, as if she were appearing on the Ed Sullivan Show, microphone in hand.

"'Give me your tired, your poor. Your huddled masses yearning to breathe free. Send these—the homeless, tempest-tossed, to me. I lift my lamp beside the golden door.'"

She really did raise the bottle above her head before she set it back down on the table. "We had to memorize that poem," she told me. "I'll loan you my camera and you can take pictures."

"Lillian, you want some Pepto-Bismol for the boy?" Sherman called to my mother.

"I want you to go into the bathroom and at least try to sit there," she told Larry. "Your mother would say the same thing."

Beads of sweat were popping onto his forehead as Larry began shuffling across the floor. At the bar, Sherman was pouring out a Pepto-Bismol cocktail. When Larry got to the bathroom, he motioned me over, so I went and stood next to him. By then, his skin was the color of the olives that my father had started dishing into little bowls on the tables.

Larry whispered, nodding toward the bathroom. "I don't want to go in there. I don't want to get polio."

I pushed him. Larry bumped into a barstool and fell onto the floor but I didn't stop. Larry could have been dead, but I stepped over his ignorant body and ran into the bathroom. I slammed the door. The seat was up, and I banged it down. I hoisted my skirt and sat, like a girl, right on the wood. Like a healthy girl who wasn't scared of polio, or of Russians, and certainly not of Sherman Carter. Not even of the boy who touched his fingers to my neck, but then gave me a quarter for the March of Dimes campaign. I flushed the toilet and came out.

Sherman had brought over the Pepto-Bismol cocktail and Larry was sipping it. He finished the glass and went into the bathroom. After, he said he felt better, but I wouldn't speak to him all the way home.

When we passed the Beth Israel Hospital, my sister asked my mother to slow the car. But it was getting dark, and we couldn't tell for sure which was the children's wing.

At school the next morning, Larry acted as if going to the Central Ward had been his idea and too bad no one else had thought of it. He kept shaking our March of Dimes canisters to prove the rich silence our money made. Amy Siegel was so jealous she called us liars, so Ivan Plotnik grabbed the can from Larry's hand and squinted at the slot to make sure the inside was stuffed with real money and not spitballs.

When Miss Powderly came in, we all took our seats. She hung her coat on the back of the door and began the Lord's Prayer. The bus to the Statue of Liberty wasn't due for a while, so we began the day in our usual way.

"'*Our Father, who art in heaven, hallowed be Thy name,*'" she said. "'*Thy kingdom come, Thy will be done, on earth as it is in heaven.*'"

I yawned loudly and shifted around, my back to the blackboard, watching the gerbils instead of her. I coughed and pretended to sneeze.

"'*Give us this day our daily bread, And let us forgiveth our tres-passers as we forgive those who trespass against us.*'"

I laughed aloud at the gerbils. That morning, they were feeling terrific. They were spinning faster and faster on their play wheel, healthy and happy. According to Miss Powderly, their hearts were as tiny as dimes. The wheel was a flash of silver.

"'*Lead us not into temptation, and deliver us from evil, for Thine is the kingdom, the power, and the glory forever.*' Amen."

As we slid back our chairs to stand for the Pledge of Allegiance, she narrowed her eyes.

"Debbie Tarlow. Are you sure that you want to go to the Statue of Liberty today?"

I pointed to the ample lunch my mother had packed for me, in a paper bag beneath my desk. "I'm sure," I said. "I'm all set."

"All right, then. Let us stand."

We did and put our hands on our hearts. When we finished the Pledge, Miss Powderly told us to stay standing and keep our hands where they were. I pressed mine on the strap of my sister's new camera, criss-crossed in its leather case against my chest.

"Can you feel it?" Miss Powderly said. "*Lub-dub, lub-dub.* Can you feel the beat? That's the sound of God breathing. That's the voice of Our Lord Jesus Christ inside each one of you."

Our classroom was quiet and still. The boys mostly looked down at the floor and the girls mostly looked up at the ceiling. Hannah Grabelsky, who was ultra-orthodox, picked at her cuticle so roughly a bright spot of blood appeared on her thumb. Slowly, it oozed to-ward her palm.

That's when I lifted my arm over my head and into the air, wav-ing my fingers at Miss Powderly. Let my flat chest sprout breasts as big and as obvious as Paula Eisenberg's. Let those breasts rise up like purple mountains full of majesty, like the huddled masses of our grandfathers, yearning to breathe free. Let the hair start to grow beneath my raised arm and even to grow like my mother's, *down there*—let it all grow wild as amber waves of grain. Since I couldn't stop it, proudly I'd hail it. Because no matter what happened, I would stay indivisible. So let it happen. Let it all happen.

I thought about the girl who had written that poem on the base of the Statue of Liberty. Miss Powderly hadn't mentioned a word about that poem. And I knew she would never admit that the girl was Jewish.

I kept my arm in the air and looked her straight in the eyes.

"Yesterday you told us that the heart was shaped like a fist. That it wasn't red or pointed at the bottom. Did you really mean that?"

Her glance slid right past me. She wouldn't answer my question. But all of my classmates were with me in spirit as I left my desk and walked to the window. On the back of my shoulders, I could feel all their eyes pushing me forward. Outside, a yellow bus pulled into the parking lot. Lined up in their buddy pairs, the fifth-graders held hands and filed out from our school's front door.

I lifted my sister's camera and peered through the viewer. I aimed in the direction where I thought the Statue of Liberty must be promising all of us the equal shelter of her torch. Somewhere behind me, Miss Powderly was hollering, but I ignored her and clicked a picture. Then another. It was not my mission to insult what she believed in or to convert her, either. But as the one in charge of my own body—of my arms and legs, my pointed heart, and whatever else eventually developed—I would record in full the day I proved her wrong about so many things.

Click-click.

Lub-dub.

I wanted solid evidence. I wanted physical proof.

POCAHANTAS IN
CAMELOT

Like parents everywhere, mine always worried—about taxes and money, about a possible upsurge in anti-Semitism, even about the weather—but when President Kennedy was shot, my mother also had to worry about Thanksgiving, which was only days away. That year, we were hosting the family dinner; my grandfather had suffered another stroke in September, just a week or so after Yom Kippur. My grandmother had promised to make her famous rice pudding, but with my grandfather in a wheelchair, that was all that she would be able to do. My mother was cooking the turkey and a few side dishes. My father had convinced her to buy the rest of the things we needed from Tabatchnik's.

"So stop worrying," he told her. "Everyone knows that Tabatchnik's has the best food in the world."

The "Late Show" had just come on. From my hiding place in the hall outside their bedroom, I was using their TV's bluish light to cut an old blouse into fringes. My mother had cried when she picked me up at school on Friday and my father had cursed when he came home from work, but now the President's murderer was dead, shot in the gut right in the Dallas police station, and I was hoping things might get back to normal. School would start again and I would wear the fringed blouse when I presented my report on Pocahantas. Neither of my parents knew that I was eavesdropping.

"We'll eat like kings," my father added. "Believe me, honey, your sisters will thank you for it."

"It's not the taste of the food."

My mother turned on the hot water in their bathroom and as the sink filled, she held her arms above the steam. Then she creamed

77

them clear up to her elbows. These nightly treatments kept her hands as soft as butter. "The food will cost a lot of money, and I don't like to rub my sisters' noses in it," she told him. "They know the prices that Tabatchnik charges."

"Buying a few pounds of potato salad and cole slaw isn't a crime in New Jersey," my father said when the water stopped running. He lit a cigar and settled in for the night as she pulled two taffeta dresses from her sewing kit. She had bought Marlee and me the dresses at Hahne's, Newark's nicest department store. She tore the gold labels from the collars and got into her side of bed with the sewing kit.

"You're not taking this seriously, but it is serious," she said.

The smack on the mattress was his hand, all frustration. I inched forward on the carpet and saw my mother scrounge through her sewing kit, pull out two plain white labels, and toss the gold ones in the wastebasket. She threaded a needle and started sewing the plainer labels into the collars of our new dresses. My father leaned over and put his hand on hers, so she couldn't go on without stabbing him. She took small, careful stitches and kept her eyes down as he talked to her. If the aunts happened to see the original labels, they wouldn't let her forget it.

"Honey, listen to me," my father said. "Maybe my parents, may they rest in peace, should have stayed where they were and waited for the next pogrom. Maybe your parents should have, too. No one gets out—separate but equal. Maybe your sisters would have liked that, since they're so democratic. Maybe we even should have stayed in that apartment on Schluy Street. But it's not like we live in a plantation down in Alabama or a villa in the south of France. It's not like we live in a mountainside palace in Shangri-La. We've got six rooms and a screened-in porch, plus two tiled bathrooms and a disposal in the kitchen sink. All right, we're doing well. We're doing very well. Still, it's not like we live in the White House."

My mother bit the thread between her teeth, snapped it off and walked to the window, pushing the sleeves of her nightgown up past her elbows. Outside, down on Weequahic Avenue, the last city bus of the night rumbled by and the air took on a deeper silence. From the window, she would have seen the dome of our synagogue, Beth David; the roofs of the apartment buildings where my aunts lived with their families; and maybe, to the east, the shiny glimmer of Manhattan.

"I think I'll go downstairs," she said when she turned back. "I told Edith not to come this week, what with everything that's happened."

She meant Edith James, who lived in the Central Ward, around the corner from my father's tavern. Once a week, she came to help my mother clean the house. Edith had a wonderful smell, a fragrant mustiness that I liked to think of as "cloves," although I had only read about cloves in books and had no idea what they smelled or tasted like—evidently something the gentiles poked into their hams so they wouldn't die from eating them. Edith must have been in her thirties, or even her forties, but my aunts always called her "the girl," and none of them understood why, having a girl, my mother cleaned the sterling silver by hand and often the floors, down there on her knees along with delicious, clovey Edith.

"Your sisters won't see you cleaning. They won't credit your account," my father said as he opened the *Newark Evening News* and started reading more stories about what had happened in Dallas. "They won't ease up on you because you get your hands dirty at ten o'clock at night."

But she kissed him on the cheek and headed for the stairs as I backed into the darkened hallway. When I heard her reach the kitchen, I stayed in the shadows but leaned into the banister. She was sprinkling baking soda on the sink and around the edges of the disposal. She cleaned the tiles along the sink with vinegar, and then she walked into the living room with a bottle of ammonia and two clean rags.

On the far wall, near our breakfront, there was a floor-to-ceiling mirror that was actually a knobless door leading back into the kitchen. Because the mirror was so hard to clean, we never used it as a door. But in the last few days, dust had gathered on the surface while we watched the President's funeral on TV. Now my mother sprayed ammonia all across the mirror. She rubbed one rag along the top and then, bending on her knees, she rubbed along the bottom, first in tiny circles and then in widening ones. Soon the ammonia's acrid smell had made her cry.

She kept rubbing her rag at the mirror, wiping the tears from her cheeks with the other rag. One spot on the bevel of the mirror wouldn't come clean, but when my mother rubbed some more, the glass began to gleam. She was on her knees, but I could see her face reflected perfectly, and her long fingers on the other rag, turning

79

red beneath the cream that she had carefully rubbed into them.

The next afternoon, my sister and I went with her to Bergen Street to pick up the food for Thanksgiving. After finishing at the fruit place, we paused on the sidewalk in front of Miss Vivian's Belles Modes Shoppe. Miss Vivian herself had come out of the shop and was standing with us. As children, she and my mother had gone to school together; they knew each other's families.

"Come on, Lillian. Wholesale—either one." Miss Vivian had small eyes that disappeared when she laughed and a French twist of hair whose color varied, depending on the season. That day it was a deep glowing orange, with the usual dark brown roots. "Take the plunge and I'll have my people make the alterations overnight. And for you, I'll forget about the tax. Let Uncle Sam go out and work for a living, just like everybody else."

"That black suit you sold me last year will last at least three more seasons," laughed my mother. She was holding a bag full of apples, plums, grapes and tangerines, a cornucopia she purchased twice weekly all year round, so our growing bones never would grow weak with scurvy or rickets or polio or any of a myriad of diseases. As a girl in the Great Depression, my mother hadn't tasted an orange until she was nearly grown and now fresh fruit was, to her, as valuable as medicine. "I've barely ever worn that suit."

My sister and I were standing at the windows of the Belles Modes Shoppe while my mother and Miss Vivian chatted. Marlee was snickering at a turquoise gown with pearly beads dangling from the bodice and real feathers at the hem, which I had suggested that our mother buy. I thought she'd look like Pocahantas—the feathers and the beads.

Marlee gazed dreamily at the dress on the other mannequin, a mess of frills the color of cough syrup. For three years she had worshipped our First Lady, her haute couture and slender figure, and of course her Frenchy maiden name.

"You've got a strange idea about the clothes that Pocahantas wore," she told me for the tenth time. "She didn't wear tops, for one thing. Anyway, the pink is ten times prettier and the one that Mama should buy. She'll look like Jackie, but in blonde. Jacqueline Bouvier Kennedy would never wear feathers," she added, savoring the exotic lilt of the middle syllables.

I elbowed her and my mother shifted her bag of fruit to separate us. A tangerine rolled onto the sidewalk, fell into the street, and came to a halt within an inch of the gutter, as efficiently as the eight-ball avoiding the pocket on the pool table in the back of my father's tavern.

"Jackie's not First Lady anymore," I told Marlee. "It doesn't matter what she'd wear."

"Look, girls," my mother said. "Instead of quibbling, watch this."

She reached into her shopping bag and plucked a bunch of grapes from their tiny gnarled tree. She widened her mouth and stretched her neck so that her thick blonde hair tumbled past her shoulders. She was wearing the ring that my father had bought her, and, as usual, the stones were turned inside her palm, so people wouldn't see their size. But as her hand went up to toss the grape, the ring slid around her finger and flashed blue and orange.

"Aaah," she said.

The grape hit the side of her nose and tippled along the sidewalk, as if too much sun had turned it into a tiny cask of Manischewitz wine. The second grape bounced off her forehead. She tossed the next a little higher, several inches from her, and gave a kind of hoot as she ran forward. The grape landed right on her tongue.

"Bingo."

My mother held her bag of fruit in one hand and put her other hand behind her back. She swallowed the grape and took a bow on Bergen Street. Miss Vivian munched an apple and peered along the sidewalk, as though the area might be filled with spies who would arrest her if they heard what she was saying.

"Let me tell you something, Lillian, and cut my own throat while I'm at it. Silk, chiffon, brocade or sackcloth: you could wear a house dress and still look like a million dollars."

"Stop," said my mother; she was blushing. "That's not true."

"Your mother was the most beautiful girl in all of South Side High School," Miss Vivian told us. "Next to Betty Grable, everyone wanted to look like her. Everyone still does."

For years, Miss Vivian had been Newark's uncontested fashion expert, but she wasn't telling me anything I didn't know. Like every story that I ever heard in Newark, this one was familiar. Wherever we went, people always were saying that my mother's skin was like cooled peasants' bread, that her eyes were the color of fresh celery, that her bearing was as regal as a queen's. They said she should have been a movie star or a model or a Rockette over in Manhattan at Radio City Music Hall. In the Central Ward, there were beauty contests sponsored by Rheingold, but in our part of Newark, it was common knowledge that my mother was the luckiest of the three Edelman sisters. "That Lillian really got the looks," people always said. "Lox, stock and barrel," Bernice or Elsie added if they overheard, somehow implicating my mother in a crime of birth—as if, without waiting to hear the lawyers read the will, she had stolen her own features while her plainer relatives clearly were in need of them.

But for a woman of such beauty, my mother was painfully modest. Her elegant hands, long and graceful as a pianist's, were her only vanity. Once a week, she had a manicure at the Bergen Beauty Parlor, but she never used make-up or colored her hair, and everything she wore was black or beige or white, and perfectly tailored.

Of course, Miss Vivian knew all this, just as Marlee and I did. But whenever we passed the Belles Modes Shoppe, Miss Vivian joined us in pretending otherwise.

"You'd look spectacular in either of those dresses," she said on that November day. "Oh, Lillian, just imagine. Can't you imagine?"

My mother looked up at the window—reassessing the beautiful turquoise gown, then Marlee's awful pink.

"Well," she said. "The truth is I can't see it."

"You're not even trying," I complained.

"Don't be silly," laughed my mother. "I'm always trying."

That night, I was sitting cross-legged on my bed, my Pocahantas books and papers sprawled around me, when my sister finished her shower and came into my room. Her wet hair was wrapped around six empty orange juice cans borrowed from Paula Eisenberg because my mother always squeezed our juice by hand. Marlee was carrying a horsehair crinoline by its stretched-out elastic waistband.

"Here," she said, holding it out. "You can put this around your neck when you're talking about Captain Smith. The Virginia colonists always wore those get-ups. I've seen pictures."

She dropped the crinoline on the bed and it stood up stiffly, by itself. I got off, crinkling my papers, and scrounged around my dresser drawer. Marlee plopped herself in the rocking chair near the window.

"I've got some money in here somewhere," I told her. "I can pay you."

"Don't be silly. It's a present."

I got back on my bed and sat waiting. Her face looked fuzzy through the crinoline's mesh.

"You know," she said, rocking slowly, "I really wish you'd stop calling me Marlee. I've gotten Mama and Pop to call me Marlene. And all of the relatives. You're the last hold-out."

"It's okay." I shrugged. "I don't mind."

"That's not the point."

I turned a page of a library book and stared at a drawing of Pocahantas arguing with her father, Chief Powhatan. Pocahantas looked passionate and the Chief looked pensive. In the background, surrounded by a crowd of naked Indians, Captain John Smith knelt on the ground and prayed for his life.

"What's the point?" I said.

"The point is that I don't like being called Marlee. It sounds like a little kid's name. I'm thirteen. I shouldn't have a little kid's name."

"If you think 'Marlene' sounds French or something, it doesn't," I told her. "It sounds Jewish. Marlene Shumofsky. Marlene Bluestone." I closed the book and named all the Marlenes that I knew. "Marlene Laskowitz, Paula Eisenberg's cousin. If you want to change your name, then I can't stop you. But I don't have to call you by it, either."

She came and sat behind me, twisting her neck to see my writing. She frowned as she read a few paragraphs of my report.

"I think you have that part wrong. Pocahantas didn't marry Captain John Smith. She saved his life, but she married John Rolfe. We learned all that in history."

"I learned something different. Something true." I pointed to my pile of library books. "Do you think I'd make this up? It's a report. It's not a story."

"Well, Marlene is not a story either. It happens to be my real name." She yawned as she turned to leave, the juice cans clacking on her head. "You can keep the crinoline. Just don't come complaining later on that no one warned you about Pocahantas and John Smith."

"I promise I won't do that. *Marlee.*"

When school resumed, the teachers all looked older, drawn and weary. On Wednesday morning, Mr. Broderick greeted us in dark glasses, perched tight on his nose instead of dangling from the chain he usually wore around his neck, but that day none of the jerky boys whispered "Four-Eyes" when he turned his back. Except for the principal, Mr. Broderick was the only man teacher in our school, and I had liked him ever since classes started. It wasn't his fault if he wasn't handsome. Lyndon Baines Johnson wasn't handsome either, far from it, and he had been Vice-President. Now he was the President.

That day, no one gave Mr. Broderick any trouble at all, and for the first time that autumn we said "Please" and "Thank You" at lunch without being told. In the morning, we read aloud from our history books, but mid-way through the chapter on Plymouth Rock, Mr. Broderick seemed to lose interest and switched abruptly to arithmetic; we slid our history books into our desks and no one made a wisecrack. He chalked a few subtraction problems on the blackboard and Hannah Grabelsky got the first one wrong, but he didn't notice, and no one waved a hand to point out that the little angel wasn't perfect after all.

In the afternoon, Mr. Broderick gave up on lessons and had us push our desks into a circle while we crayoned paper turkeys and cut Pilgrim hats from cardboard, talking quietly about where we had been when the President was shot. Every one of us had been outside at recess when the principal walked onto the playground and made the announcement, but everyone seemed to remember something different. Amy Siegel and Joyce Bluestone couldn't stop thinking about this little baby chipmunk they'd been watching; they said it kept running in and out of the wire diamonds of the fence. Larry Eisenberg said his basketball seemed to spin around the hoop's orange rim for hours—but as usual, this wasn't true; I was the one who threw that basketball. I kept watching it circle the rim, and I kept thinking that Dr. Krumbeigel's news could change—that everything he said could be undone, the way Pocahantas had thought that Captain Smith was doomed to death and then gloriously won his freedom for him.

Mr. Broderick wore those dark glasses all day long. Above the hissing   radiators at the window, the sun had disappeared and the sky was turning colorless. "It will snow," he told us when we went out for recess, and no one pointed out that it was still too early in the season. "Can you smell it?" We just stood around him, breathing in, and didn't go near the places we had been the previous Friday.

At the end of the afternoon, I went into the supply closet, changed into my fringed blouse, and gave my report on Pocahantas. When it came time to explain about Captain John Smith, I slid my sister's crinoline around my neck. After I finished the marriage scene, my classmates applauded and I took three bows.

When everyone stopped clapping, I waited for Mr. Broderick's words of praise.

"Well, Debbie. You certainly read your speech very well," he told me. "Your penmanship could use some work, but you have excellent enunciation. So I'm sorry to say that you've gotten the facts wrong." Mr. Broderick removed his glasses as he told me this, and like everyone else in the room, I looked at his red, rheumy eyes and wondered what he possibly could mean.

"Pocahantas saved Captain Smith from being murdered," I explained. "Her father, Chief Powhatan, was all set to kill him. He had his hatchet ready and the funeral pyre was burning when she ran up and put her own neck to the blade."

I wasn't sure about the pyre part, but had seen the word in print, and figured it would stop him. "That's it," I told him. "That's what happened."

"Yes, I know." Mr. Broderick nodded. "And her courageous act did save his life. But Captain Smith didn't marry Pocahantas."

And that's when he said that Captain Smith had handed Pocahantas over to John Rolfe, just as my sister warned me. He said that John Rolfe took the Indian princess back to England, dressed her in a satin gown, and got the Queen to call her "Lady Rebecca." And Pocahantas never again saw her beloved Virginia or heard her true name spoken.

By then, the dismissal bell had rung. I was smiling as my classmates raced away—I assumed that Mr. Broderick must be joking. But when the halls had quieted and we were left alone, something in his face confused me all over again. And then he repeated what he had said: that only for the sake of peace between her tribe and the colonists had Pocahantas laid her yearning throat beneath her father's hatchet while the tom-toms begged for war.

I stood near the radiators and watched Mr. Broderick gather up his things. Finally, I said, "Then you don't think Pocahantas saved John Smith because of love?"

But even I could hear the quaver in my voice as I waited for him to take back what *he'd* said. But, of course, teachers never did that. Once they said a thing, then that was it. If a teacher told you ten times ten was ninety-nine, you were supposed to believe it. And Four-Eyes was no different.

"I could have sworn the book I read said something about that," I told him.

Mr. Broderick turned off the lights. "I'm sorry, Debbie," he repeated. "I know you read a book. I know how hard you worked."

In fact, I'd read three library books, and I didn't believe a word that Mr. Broderick was telling me. I was sure Pocahantas had wound up in a Virginia teepee with Captain Smith, not in a damp English manor with dull John Rolfe. Or, if somehow a cruel twist of fate had really trapped her on a boat in the Atlantic, then I figured she must have died of a broken heart at sea.

The next morning was Thanksgiving, a cold and glassy sky. By afternoon, the bay windows had frosted in the dining rooms along Keer Avenue. The oaks and maples were completely bare now, and only the hills of dead leaves raked to the curbs proved that they had ever been different.

By the end of the meal, I had spilled gravy and a glob of cranberry sauce down the front of my new taffeta dress. Our table was strewn with empty plates. We had finished Tabatchnik's potato salad, cole slaw, sour tomatoes, chopped liver, three kinds of breads, all kinds of pickles. My mother's home-cooked turkey was picked to the bone. Our crystal fruit bowl was half-empty.

At the middle of the table, my grandfather sat in the portable wheelchair that my mother had bought to keep at our house. My grandmother sat beside him, cutting his food into tiny pieces and holding the fork to his mouth. My father and Uncle Nat sat at either end. My mother's sisters and their families filled the seats between.

By then, my cousin Kitty was chomping on her second plum. "Kennedy started the Peace Corps," she was saying.

"His fancy-shmancy father was a bootlegger," said my grandmother. "A peasant who dreamed of being a czar."

"When I'm old enough, I'm joining it," said Kitty.

"I might do that too," said Marlee. "Or I might be a stewardess. I'd like to go to Africa, or South America, and do some good for mankind. *Peut-etre* Bechuanaland," she added dreamily. "Or Sierra Leone. I could use my French there."

"Let the younger generation forge ahead and try to change the world," said Uncle Nat. "Let them go ahead and root for the Commies. Let them learn the hard way."

My cousin Dickie finished his second plum and started on his third. "Kennedy wasn't a saint. Look at the Bay of Pigs. Look at southeast Asia."

Marlee rolled her eyes and elbowed him. "Look at Alan Shepherd and John Glenn."

"Careful with those plums," Aunt Elsie warned Dickie. "They have more sugar than you think. They'll rot out your teeth." She turned to the oldest aunt, Bernice. "Actually I'm surprised that Lillian has any fruit left for us," she said. "Last week when I stopped over here, she was polishing the silver while her girl sat at the table munching a fresh apricot, calm as you please."

"Edith," I said. "Her name is Edith."

Aunt Bernice took off her shoes and rubbed her feet. From time to time, she stood all day on her aching arches and handled the cash register at the grocery store in the Central Ward where Heshie and Lou were partners. Later, she said, her feet always swelled up like a pair of salamis.

"If you want to marry a *shvartzer* then you don't have to go to Africa," she told my sister. "Just walk across South Orange Avenue. Plenty of *shvartzers* on South Orange Avenue."

My mother brushed some hair from her face with the palm of her hand. A golden strand caught in her ring but instead of untangling it, she yanked. She pulled the strand free and let it drift onto the carpet. "That's not funny," she said. "Not at all."

Aunt Bernice glanced at her and winked at Elsie, who occasionally answered the phone for Dr. Blumenthal, our dentist. Luckily for her, Dr. Blumenthal was getting old and couldn't take many patients. "Look at her face! That beautiful face!" Aunt Bernice said. "All twisted up like a loaf of challah."

"Please don't call me a pronoun," my mother said. "You know I hate that."

Nat pulled a few cigars from his pocket and got up to distribute them to the men. To my father he said, "Here Vic, try one of these. Havana—smuggled up just last week." He took a long puff. "Jack Kennedy may have had *cajones* but he couldn't have been a true connoisseur, or he'd have used kid gloves with Castro."

"You're confusing JFK with Eisenhower," my father said to Dickie. "Ike's the one who sent the first advisors out to Asia. Although, of course, he had his reasons. But I'll take bets that Johnson gets us out of there by winter."

"Actually," mused Marlee, "I think I'd rather go to Paris."

My father's remark about Eisenhower had made Aunt Elsie indignant. "How ridiculous! Kennedy had a full head of hair. Everyone in that family has terrific hair, even the children. Tragedy doesn't change good blood."

In the kitchen, a geyser of steam shot to the ceiling. My mother went in and came back with the kettle and a platter of strudel. She poured the tea and coffee, but instead of sipping hers, she held a hand above the steam until her flesh was damp, then turned her palm and stared at it.

"I feel so sorry for Caroline and John-John," Kitty said. "They're nearly orphans now."

Heshie unknotted his tie and loosened his belt. "Johnson is good for the Jews," he said. "If he can just keep a lid on the *shvartzers* ."

My father rolled his cigar between his hands and stared at it. "Try saying 'Negroes,' Hesh."

"Maybe the ones who go into your tavern are Negroes. The ones who come into our grocery store are *shvartzers.* "

"Their money is as green as yours or mine. So you ought to call them what they want to be called."

"Maybe if I had your luck, then I could afford to."

"At least call them Negroes when you're sitting in my house, eating the food that their money paid for."

Nat sipped his glass of tea and wiped the corners of his mouth with a napkin, first one side and then the other. He rested his elbows on the table, angled in his forearms, and let his index fingers touch. At the base of the triangle formed by his hands, his thumbs were also touching.

"I'd say that Vic is offering a square deal, Hesh. If I were you, I'd take it. Of course, I don't have any particular feelings on the subject of Negroes, one way or the other. But you know I'm prone to indigestion. It's the cost of doing business, but nevertheless—when I'm with my family, I would like a little peace. I don't think I'm asking too much, really. I don't think that I'm being unreasonable."

"Sure, Nat," said Heshie. "Sorry. Sure."

Aunt Bernice snatched away Dickie's next plum. "That's enough with the plums," she told him. "You're always getting diarrhea from Lillian's wonderful plums. Last week I had to pump him full of Kaopectate," she announced to the rest of us. "All night I was up with him because of Lillian's delicious nutritious fruit."

Dickie shuddered and put his face in his hands. My mother stopped eating her strudel as I got up from the table and wandered to the mirrored door. Neither of my aunts realized that it was actually a door and I was standing there, thinking about how dazzled and jealous they would be if they knew, when my Aunt Bernice turned back to my sister. "Don't you worry about Jackie," she said. "With her looks and her money, she'll find another man in no time."

My mother stood, leaning over the table as she clinked plates and glasses, then carried away a teetering stack. Spoons and forks fell to the carpet. But instead of picking them up, she kicked them away and kept walking. And just as I was swinging through the beveled glass to show the aunts that things weren't always what they thought they were, or at least could possibly be different, I heard a scream, my mother's scream, and saw her arm in the sink, and the kitchen tiles turned into a singe of splattered red—my mother's blood.

All those tiles, sparkling and hand-cleaned with vinegar, bright with blood, down the hallway and out into the yard, where she ran screaming, trailing all that blood. I stayed frozen where I was, imagining the tips of manicured fingers as they swirled around and around in our stainless steel disposal, around and around and around, like my basketball on its orange rim at school. Behind me on the mirrored door, my own ten fingerprints were clear as maps.

The relatives began to yell and knock chairs over as I stood frozen, thinking: now I'll have to clean the mirror by myself. And I'll never get it clean. Around and around and around. I'll have to clean everything myself now. And I'll never get it clean. Around and around and around.

And later, after my father had disappeared with her moaning in the front seat of our car, I scrubbed and scrubbed my fingerprints from the mirrored door while the aunts tried to make me stop. I wouldn't go in the kitchen, where my mother kept the ammonia and the rags, so I used water from the crystal pitcher on the table and two linen napkins. My aunts' sobbing sickened me; I wouldn't cry.

The bevel at the mirror's bottom was the trickiest part and for that I knelt, my back towards all of them. And in the reflection of the glass I watched my sister say that they could all go home, that being thirteen now, she was old enough to stay with me.

The portable wheelchair my mother had bought to keep at our house for my grandfather was sleek and gleaming, with padded sheepskin seat and armrests—"top of the line" my father had said just that morning, while he personally oiled the wheels. When my relatives' headlights had faded and Keer Avenue was silent, I pushed it through the living room, out onto the lawn, down to the sidewalk. The big wheels made a quiet whoosh, barely any sound at all. The cracked and tilted sidewalk might have been a newly laid red carpet, so easily did I travel over it.

The front door opened, and my sister came out with my jacket. Along Keer Avenue, the silhouettes of the oaks and maples were beginning to take shape against the yellow moon, but the most powerful light stayed inside with our neighbors. Through their windows I could see the Siegels and the Eisenbergs relaxing in their living rooms, still dressed in their holiday clothing. The ultra-orthodox Grabelsky girls were helping their mother clear the table as their father watched the news on TV. Two doors down, Mr. and Mrs. Rymaruk and their sons sat laughing in their kitchen.

When I got to the corner, I looked down Bergen Street. But my father was gone and the Beth Israel Hospital was way up Lyons Avenue, too far away to see. My sister tossed me my jacket and walked a few feet behind me.

"Smell that air," she said. "It'll snow."

Our neighbors' lights blinked off, the first few stars came out, and the metal rims on the wheelchair numbed my fingers. After that, my sister pushed me. We were on our fourth time around the block when my father's car came down Bergen Street and turned the corner toward us. By then, the night air had grown as sharp as glass.

The next afternoon, he took us to the Beth Israel. My mother was sitting up in the bed, her hand bandaged to twice its size. I avoided looking at her, but my sister went over and sat near her feet until my mother told her to come closer. I fiddled with my jacket zipper and, from the corner of my eye, watched Mama stroke her palm and try to talk to her. My sister wasn't saying much.

"Don't you worry," Mama said. "It's my left hand, not my right, and just the tips of the last two fingers. The doctors say that, except for the nails, we'll never notice the difference."

The police had come that night, after my father got home from the hospital. They had taken apart our garbage disposal and brought the pieces to the Beth Israel. But all the doctors found there were some half-ground turkey bones and her ring. The doctors had said that flesh could not survive those blades.

My mother winked at my father, who was standing at the window, fiddling with the shade. Outside, the sky was tough and heavy, cold blue with streaks of white. The snow still hadn't started.

"Maybe there's a silver lining," she said. "Maybe I can get the woman at the beauty parlor to give me twenty per cent off on my manicures."

My father's big shoulders flinched, but he kept his features steady as he fiddled with that shade. After a while, I didn't have much choice, and I had to go to my mother. Actually, my sister made me do it. She stood up and smoothed down her skirt; then she came and pulled my socks back to my knees. She took my hand and toured me all around the room, as if she thought we were in Europe or Africa or somewhere exotic. But then she showed me the tiny bottles of mouthwash and baby powder lined up on the sink, the rented television in the corner that looked exactly like ours at home, the bulletin board where my father had tacked my crayoned turkey.

And then we were sitting on the bed, on either side of my mother's elbows. My sister had taken the hand side and let me have the other, but I could see that the gauze on my mother's arm was clean. No blood anywhere.

"What are you thinking?" I said, to any of them.

No one answered. My mother closed her celery eyes. In a quiet voice she said, "Oh, nothing. I wasn't really thinking of anything."

Then, because she never had been able to pretend and because we all knew anyway, she exhaled and said, "I was thinking about my sisters. I was thinking how different things would be if they wished me well."

When she leaned back and eased her arms out against the pillow, I took it as an invitation to duck under. On her other side, so did my sister. There, enfolded in her, several moments passed. Not a sound. My mother's skin was pale but smooth and smelled as fresh as bread.

Finally, I said, "Things would be different, Mama. So different that you can't imagine it."

And then I told her how, at first, Pocahantas thought she couldn't survive without John Smith, or her family in Virginia. I told how, at night, she cried herself to sleep and dreamed of maize and wild cranberries. How, eventually, she had new friends and children of her own, who helped her to go on.

And she began to love her life. Periodically, she dressed in silks and satins and went to meet the Queen for tea. In Buckingham Palace, they spoke of books and music, the latest restaurants, and the excesses of fashion. At dusk, she often rode her chestnut mare along Pall Mall's calming paths. John Rolfe adored her and, content together, they lived for many years and knew their grandchildren, and great-grandchildren.

I had reached the great-great-grandchildren and even Marlene seemed to be transported, when something in my mother began to make a steady beat within her body, like a heart, or tiny drum. My father kept on fiddling with that shade until the whole thing snapped up against the window frame. The afternoon had faded now, deepened into dusk. Above Newark's old familiar buildings, I saw Pocahantas galloping, galloping safely, through the English mist. She wore a beaded turquoise riding gown and held the reins lightly in her perfect fingers. And on the back of her blonde crown, a pillbox hat bobbed lightly. My eyes began to sting, and finally to tear, as if God was somewhere up there on His knees, cleaning the whole universe in preparation for the colder months that seemed so certain, so inevitable, now.

THE WIDOWER
VISARRION

Even before the Newark riots, my mother started to talk about leaving the city where we'd all been born. In those days, on Keer Avenue, suburban dreams were not unusual. For a long time, the Siegel family had had its eye on Livingston, where there already was a Jewish mortuary. The Eisenbergs preferred to dream of Springfield, with its landscaped cul-de-sacs of look-alike split-levels. Even the ultra-orthodox Grabelskys hoped to move some day, although they couldn't agree on where, and argued constantly. But, alone among our neighbors, my mother chose to dream about Short Hills. Only fifteen minutes from Newark straight up South Orange Avenue, there were no signs to mark its start or end: if you didn't know, you didn't belong.

Nearly every night that winter, she sat in the kitchen with the real-estate section of the *Newark News* spread open on the Formica table. Sometimes while she scanned the ads, she squinted, with her eyebrow tweezers darting at a plump fresh capon. Every so often, she dabbed Wesson on the hairy yellow skin; plucking was easier if you oiled lightly. My grandmother also oiled and, like her, my mother kept a vague version of Kosher (bacon was okay, pork and ham never) because botulism and other diseases were carried in gentile food. Practicing or non-practicing Jews, none of us wanted to die that way.

I sat across from her and sipped a mug of hot chocolate, warming my hands over the steam. My sister sat between us. From time to time, my mother jabbed the tweezers at an ad and motioned Marlene to circle it with the Magic Marker. Outside, the season's first snow was gathering speed. A layer of frost was starting to build on the window.

My sister leaned over my mother's shoulder and read some ads aloud.

"'French provincial feeling set on an English garden corner lot.' 'Pristine ranch on quiet cul-de-sac with built-in swimming pool,'" Marlene read. "Wow! In the summer, I could have a pool party!"

"Kids are always drowning in swimming pools. Try reading the headlines," I told her.

That autumn, my mother had found a frame colonial that was put up for sale by its owners. But the colonial had been sold to someone else before my father could take time off from work to go see it. "There'll be another house," he had said when he finally came in that night, and my mother told him. "We'll work through a realtor."

It was nearly my bedtime and my mother had gone to the stove to heat up his dinner.

"It's past nine o'clock," she said without turning around. "I thought that you'd been killed."

Only one gentile family lived on Keer Avenue. The Rymaruks were some sort of Eastern Orthodox, same old Christian to us, and for the most part they kept to themselves. Mr. Rymaruk worked at the distillery along the river; it was rumored that he belonged to a union. The older son, John, hoped to become a priest and the younger one, Gregory, played quarterback for the parochial school attached to the Rymaruks' church, which was in a different part of Newark. On the Sunday morning in October when their mother was hit by a car, the news reached us almost accidentally. Hannah Grabelsky's father happened to be driving through that part of Newark and saw the ambulance, the police cars, the parishioners keening in the street.

People on our block always had been polite to the Rymaruks, but after that, nobody knew what to say to the father and the sons. The huge and random nature of their loss seemed a violation of all that we believed in: life contained a certain logic, an inherent sense; hard work would be rewarded; mothers survived, *no matter what*, to raise their children.

Before then, I had always kept my distance from the Rymaruks. But now, I began crossing the street to avoid passing their house. If pale, myopic Hannah Grabelsky was tagging along, she had no choice but to follow.

Hannah was a quiet girl, well-mannered and studious, but a rich source for my pity. On Keer Avenue, the fathers gave money to B'nai B'rith. When the mothers got itchy from being home all day long, they volunteered for Hadassah; the older kids collected for Israeli trees. So for a while that winter, I tried to be good to Hannah Grabelsky. Convinced that she had nothing I wanted, I could afford to be generous. First of all, her clothes were awful, always brown or gray or a terrible shade of yellowish green and, like her mother, even on hot days she wore too many layers of them. Her hair was no darker than mine, but wild and wiry; every morning, Mrs. Grabelsky spent nearly an hour forcing it into tight, thick braids.

Hannah stuttered. At school when we learned penmanship, our teacher had forced her to switch the pencil from her left hand to her right. "Wh-wh-why are we going th-this way, D-D-Debbie?" she asked me.

It irritated me that Hannah found it so hard to see what was obvious. For in addition to the other oddities that kept him different, Mr. Rymaruk had turned into a *widower*. The word had an unnatural ring, being too bulky with syllables, as if invented for unusual circumstances, and in the first flush of crisis. I imagined being a widower as a condition peculiar to the various denominations of Christianity, or maybe to those who joined up with unions, because in Jewish families, the men always died first. Orthodox, Conservative, even Reform, we mostly owned our own businesses or aimed towards that practical goal, and we mostly had widows when someone died.

My mother started visiting Mr. Rymaruk in December, a month or so after she decided on Short Hills. On the guise of borrowing a stick of butter or a cup of sugar, she put on her coat and boots, tossed a scarf around her neck, and applied a touch of lipstick, which she rarely used. "You're in charge," she told my sister. Late at night, when my father came home, he would ask how Mr. Rymaruk was doing, and my mother would report that he seemed better, or he'd had a set-back, and I never saw the butter or the sugar she had gone to get.

As soon as our neighbors learned about her decision to buy in Short Hills, they blamed the new widower for converting my mother to a perverse way of thinking. Nothing else, they said, could explain opting for a town like that, so far in spirit if not distance from everything we knew and were. When my mother sent me to the bakery, I overheard them talking. By then, the windows had frosted so thickly I couldn't see the cupcakes lined up in their trays. Inside, sweat dripped from the glass. "What's wrong with Springfield or West Orange?" Mrs. Siegel was asking Mrs. Eisenberg. "What's wrong with Livingston?"

And in truth, the surviving Rymaruks were well taken care of; they didn't need my mother's small gestures of sympathy. Once a week, Mr. Rymaruk's spinster sister arrived to clean the furniture, blue the laundry, iron the shirts. His aged mother stopped by every Monday, lugging saucepans and skillets, ladles and strainers. She cooked until evening, so that her own flesh and blood would have food for the week. At the time, this seemed to explain why my own mother brought them neither cakes nor casseroles on her visits, but asked for things we didn't need and never received.

She was on the kitchen phone with my father one afternoon late in January when I came home from school. Outside, the snow was to my knees, and falling heavily. I stomped my boots as she twisted the cord around and around on her forearm. After a while, she sighed into the receiver. "For God's sake, Vic," she said. "If you close early one night, that doesn't mean we land in the poorhouse."

When she hung up, she went to the stairs, calling my sister to come help her start supper. I sat at the table and opened my arithmetic workbook. I knew that my mother especially hated these long winter nights, just the three of us alone in the house.

"When is Pop coming home?" I asked.

My mother clinked pots and pans, started water to boil. "The stores might be closed in the morning if this snow keeps up," she said. "After supper, I'll run over to the Rymaruks' and borrow a few things."

"When I finish my homework, I might go with you," I told her. "I've got a lot, though. I can't guarantee when I'll be done. It'll probably take me all night."

Above the sink, the window had become a dark mirror. My mother caught her reflection and patted her hair, adjusted her collar.

The Widower Visarrion

"That's not necessary, Sweetie. I know how you feel about the Rymaruks. It's no secret. Nothing's a secret on this block," she added.

She sliced some potatoes, opened some cans at the sink. I tackled a few arithmetic problems, but got nowhere with the fractions. There was nothing I could say to stop my mother, because we both knew that I had been afraid of the Rymaruks for as long as we had lived two doors down from them.

The morning we moved to Keer Avenue, my grandmother had driven from her house on Renner Avenue to help us. She was in our new dining room unpacking our china when a woman in a long-sleeved black dress crossed our front lawn, carrying a yellow sponge cake wrapped in wax paper. On her way past the movers, the woman lowered her eyes and kissed her fingertips. Then, looking up, she touched them to the tarnished *mezuzah* that the old owners had nailed on the door frame.

It was a sweltering day in late August. I scratched a mosquito bite on my forearm—that dark dress made me feel itchy just looking at it. On her way to help my grandmother, my sister swatted my hand. Every apartment or house I'd ever been in had *mezuzahs* in the doorways; that wasn't unusual in the least. But except for my grandfather, I had never seen anyone kiss them, never anyone whose hair wasn't silver or white, whose voice was unaccented, who had been born here.

"I'm Harriet Grabelsky."

In the living room, our new neighbor stood with my mother, their backs to the floor fan. My sensible mother was dressed in striped pedal-pushers and an old sleeveless blouse, the ends knotted a few inches above her slim waist. That morning, she had pinned up her long golden hair. Loose tufts blew onto her forehead. But Mrs. Grabelsky's hair didn't flutter.

"She's wearing a wig," Marlene whispered. "All the ultra-orthodox women do that once they're married. Underneath, she's bald. Bald as an eagle."

This tidbit of exotica struck me as fascinating, but possibly untrue. Still, my sister was older, worldly in ways I only could envy. Nor had I ever met an ultra-orthodox person. My grandfather was orthodox, but no one else in our family was religious at all, although my grandmother lit candles for her dead and sent clothing to relatives still in Odessa. Sometimes their letters arrived with holes cut from the middle—the story's best part excised by the censor, crumpled or burned, forever gone.

"The Eisenbergs live over there." Mrs. Grabelsky was pointing out our bay window. "They have a girl and a boy."

On Keer Avenue, the front doors of a few houses were starting to open. Women in flowered house dresses waved to each other as they plucked the morning's newspapers from the trim lawns and sidewalks. Here and there, a child emerged and jumped on a bicycle or began playing hop-scotch. While the movers brought in the loveseat, I wondered which children would become my best friends, which ones my enemies.

"In that house, the Siegels, two daughters," Mrs. Grabelsky was saying. "Over there the Bluestones, a girl and boy. That one's the Finkelsteins'. They're retired, their children are grown. The Salzmans live there, they have twin boys. My husband and I also have twins—daughters, and another one younger." She smiled when she realized I was listening. "My Hannah is your age. I hope that you'll be friends." Sighing, she turned back to my mother. "God willing, we'll be blessed with a son some day soon."

My mother bent down to our picnic basket, which was packed with small cartons of juice and milk, set among frozen cans of Scotch Ice. Not a single crumb or drop of fluid would enter the refrigerator until my grandmother had certified it sufficiently immaculate. "How about a nice cold drink?" my mother asked. "Or would you like a piece of fruit?"

"Neither, thank you," said Mrs. Grabelsky.

At the dining room table, my grandmother, who saved everything in case of another Great Depression or a pogrom, unwrapped a platter and flattened the newspaper into a pile, thrusting her chin toward our new neighbor. "Nothing's ever pure enough for ones like that," she muttered.

Across the street, another woman left her house and came to our front door. My mother let her in and Mrs. Grabelsky introduced us all to Mrs. Siegel. A few minutes later, Mrs. Grabelsky said she must go home to start preparing for the Sabbath. At sundown all her work had to be done—the cooking and cleaning, the washing and ironing. On her way out, she pointed at the house two doors down from ours.

"That one's the Rymaruks'. They're Ukrainian."

The china cups in my grandmother's hands tinkled dangerously. Mouthing three words without saying them outright, she waved at my sister and me. For a moment, I thought she was playing Charades. But then she spoke.

"Come. Right now."

I jumped. My grandmother didn't play games, and she didn't require volume to make a strong impression. In the kitchen, she leaned down and clutched our forearms. Her black eyes were burning. Her bluish hair glinted like metal.

"Be very careful when you walk past that house," she told us. "Never turn your backs, not for one second. Don't ever let them feed you. Don't even drink their water."

The door to the kitchen swung open.

"For God's sake." My mother was waving a wad of cash that my father had given her before leaving that morning. She had just settled the bill with the movers. "We're in America. I understand, Ma, I do. I try. But can't you control yourself for their sakes? Ma, they're *children*."

Gram's head snapped up. She unclenched our forearms and took a step forward. I felt relieved that the knives, even those meant for butter, weren't yet unpacked.

"Don't tell me 'children,'" she said. "I was fifteen years old when I came on the boat. Some things they're safer knowing than not knowing."

I looked down at the flesh above my elbow. The print of her fingers had left five deep red marks.

Later that night, when I awakened sweating and screaming about Nazis, my mother called her.

There was a full moon that evening. My parents' new bedroom was lined with stacked cartons casting odd shadows. Only one lamp was plugged in, its shade tilted up to give better light. The clock on the dresser showed long past midnight. My father still wasn't home.

I laid under the sheets, listening to my mother argue in Yiddish with *her* mother. No one had ever sat down to teach me that language, but the meanings of the most interesting words always came clear from the tone in which they were uttered: *meshuginer* for confoundingly crazy; *shnorrer* for someone lazy or cheap; *shmuck* both for the penis and for a man you didn't like, who, in his failure at being a *mensch,* a fine human being, turned into nothing but that part of the body.

After a while, my mother switched into English.

"It may interest you to know that the Rymaruks' family hid Jews," she told my grandmother. "Not that that's the point."

My mother was aware of the ennobling truth about the Rymaruks because Mrs. Grabelsky, who knew the family a little better than anyone else on the block, had told her. For a few dollars each Sabbath, one of the Rymaruk boys turned the lights on and off for her own family, since the Grabelskys were forbidden all forms of toil from sundown Friday to sundown Saturday. That first afternoon, after Mrs. Grabelsky left our house to prepare for the Sabbath, Mrs. Siegel had confirmed the information. Then she told my mother about Mr. and Mrs. Grabelsky. "Harriet's family never cared for Mickey," she said. "They felt he wouldn't amount to anything, saw it early on. His people are from the Bukovina. They're even darker than your Debbie—darker than gypsies."

My mother got up and put some fruit on the table, then ripped open a carton, found the kettle, and started water to boil. "Go ahead and do what you need to," Mrs. Siegel told her. So my mother started lining the cabinets with Con-tac paper and unpacking our dishes while Mrs. Siegel talked and sipped her tea. Pretty soon I could tell that my mother had stopped listening. She was lifting things from cartons, but holding onto them too long, as if she couldn't decide if she really wanted to set our things down, or to pack them back up.

The winter my mother started house-hunting in Short Hills turned out to give us the worst storm that anyone could remember. The snow was so dense and steady that white was nearly all I saw: endless white that turned Keer Avenue to a landscape nearly rural, masked in huge drifts the size of hills. The night it began, I stood at the kitchen window and watched my mother make her way across our yard, past the Eisenbergs', to the Rymaruks'. The branches of the oak and maple trees were as white as bones. The frozen ground was slick with ice and I felt she walked too quickly, nearly carelessly, her left arm bent, her head low against the wind.

By late evening, the roads were so bad that my father spent two hours driving the mile or so from the Central Ward. Because he hadn't started out until long after my mother told him was sensible, by the time he pulled into the driveway she was back from the Rymaruks' and on the phone with the Newark police. She went straight upstairs without saying hello, and my father had to heat his own supper.

The next morning, school was canceled. It took Marlene and me nearly an hour to get into all of the clothes that my mother insisted we wear to go out and play. When I finally waddled to where I thought the curb must be, Hannah Grabelsky was there with her father, the two of them squinting at the blinding white from behind their steamed eyeglasses and grounded by four of the ugliest galoshes I had ever seen. My mother had made me a thermos of hot chocolate and in a burst of fellow-feeling, I offered Hannah a sip. Then I let her follow me to the corner, where Amy Siegel and her friends had gathered to watch the arrival of the plow trucks.

Large and powerful as tanks, the plows pushed Keer Avenue's snow along the curbs and back onto the sidewalks, and the men started shoveling all over again. My father wouldn't hear of taking even one day off from work and I felt proud of his ferocious effort. I considered Mr. Rymaruk far less able, clearing only a foot or so of sidewalk to every several feet of Pop's. Instead of bending safely from the knees, Mr. Rymaruk kept his back erect; I thought it likely he would have a heart attack, with no wife to warn him on the proper way to bend and lift.

Mr. Grabelsky wasn't accomplishing much at all. After a while, he stabbed his shovel into a snowdrift and walked to his driveway, where his car was buried. Somehow he managed to back out and get away, great chunks of snow flying from the hood and windshield as the car inched down Keer Avenue.

"What on earth is *she* doing?" Amy Siegel asked me.

In the middle of the street, Hannah was racing after her father, skidding and tripping, waving her arms and stuttering something we couldn't understand. When her father's car was out of sight, she stopped. Her hat had flown off, into a snowdrift.

The Law of Return

That morning, Mrs. Grabelsky hadn't fixed her braids, and as Hannah trudged back up the street toward the rest of us, her hair frizzed out as wildly as her mother's wig always stayed stiff in place.

Amy pulled off her mittens and shrieked as she lifted her hands to Hannah's head. "*Shvartzer*-hair!"

"You're exaggerating," said Judy Bluestone.

"Then you touch it," Amy said.

"Don't let them," I said in a voice strong enough so Hannah could hear, yet low enough that the others couldn't. "If you don't want them to, don't let them. It's your hair. You don't have to."

But Hannah looked at me with an expression as bland as my grandmother's rice pudding while the other girls gathered round, forming a gauntlet of lifted palms.

"I g-g-guess it's okay," Hannah told them, and I felt a stab of the anger that the targets of our altruism so often inspire when they decide their own fates. Hannah's lack of appreciation literally caused a pain in my chest. It was my heart, hardening against her.

The next morning, Mrs. Siegel called our house. My mother cradled the phone in her neck and yanked up the blinds, stretching the telephone cord across the kitchen. She listened for a minute or two, looking out. Then she said, "Maybe I'll run over there."

Marlene stood at the counter, reading the real estate ads in the newspaper. It was Saturday, but as usual my father was in his work clothes. I got my cereal and poured my juice as my mother hung up the phone and put on her coat and boots.

"Where's the fire?" my father asked her.

"According to Estelle Siegel's morning report, the Grabelskys didn't go to *shul* this morning," my mother said. "I admit—for them, that does seem odd."

I went to the window and looked out. Next door, Hannah's house seemed the same as usual. Two doors down, Mr. Rymaruk was in his yard, shoveling his driveway.

"Go around the front," I told my mother. "The yard's all ice. You'll fall and break your neck."

"Don't be silly. I do it all the time. Five minutes," she told my father.

After she left, Marlene started reading the ads aloud. "'Mock English Tudor with Japanese rock garden and finished basement on hilly corner.' 'Center-hall brick colonial with distinguished heritage on wooded lakeside lot.'" When the traitoress came and sat next to me, I moved my chair away. "If it's Japanese, then that proves it's junky," I said.

My father stayed at the counter, looking out the window as he sipped his coffee. With his back to me he said, "You know, Sweetie, up in Short Hills, you'll be able to ride your bike in the street."

"I like the sidewalk. The sidewalk is fine. You can get killed, riding in the street. Look at what happened to Mrs. Rymaruk. And she was only walking."

The back door banged open. My mother returned, untying her scarf. She put an arm on my shoulder and used her other palm to wipe my milk mustache.

"Mickey's gone," she told my father.

"Gone? What do you mean, 'Mickey's gone'?"

"He ran off, that's what I mean. He left. He's a man with two legs, and a livelihood, and he left. Harriet asked me to call her family. She didn't have the strength."

My mother switched to Yiddish as she walked my father to his car, interrupting herself only to tell me to stay in the house. So I sneaked out the back and crouched at the frozen azalea bushes, straining to listen. But my parents had lowered their voices. I couldn't hear a word. I couldn't even tell if they were talking about Mickey Grabelsky.

It didn't take long for more complete information to fill the chill air on Keer Avenue. It was true that Mr. Grabelsky had abandoned his family—a bulletin stunning enough. More shocking was the update on the news. Hannah's father had run off with someone the neighbors began calling "a common floozy."

The verdict was swift and harsh. Mickey Grabelsky had turned into a lunatic, a madman with no endearing habits and therefore no Yiddish word to describe him, a monster who deserved to fry in the electric chair, preferably with his naked *shmuck* soaking wet. Meanwhile, Harriet Grabelsky ascended to the role of martyr, because after a few weeks she allowed him to visit the girls, when really what she should have done was purchased a shotgun and blown off his head. Blown off the floozy's head, too. Nobody would blame Mrs. Grabelsky, not one bit. In fact, she'd deserve a civic award for the act. "A gentile floozy," I heard the neighbors say one day in late March when my mother sent me to the bakery for a loaf of rye bread. "Of course, that's like saying pizza pie. Repeating the same words."

No one seemed surprised that the Grabelsky apples were starting to fall near the tree. Cindy, one of the raven-haired twins my sister's age, had been spotted smoking cigarettes with a trio of hoods in greased-down hair and tight black pants. Naomi, an oddly unappealing version of Cindy—a kind of forerunner of Hannah—was running around with a drop-out from the parochial school the Rymaruk boys attended. The biggest news was that the previous weekend, Mr. Grabelsky had had the nerve to come for his daughters with the floozy plunked right beside him in the front seat of his car. By nightfall, when they returned, all three girls were wearing brand-new mohair sweaters that the floozy gave them.

By then, the worst of the winter was past us and the air was milder than it had been in months. The icicles on the eaves of the houses were melting and stubby. At the Siegels', Amy and her friends sat on her stoop as they watched Gregory Rymaruk drag his family's garbage cans through the gray slush to the curb.

"Mr. Grabelsky and his floozy never can get married. I heard my mother tell your mother that they have to live in sin," Amy was explaining, as if Sin were a town like Short Hills, where no one in his right mind would want to venture.

Judy Bluestone nodded. "And rot in hell. That's what my mother says. Only a miracle can save those poor twins."

Gregory Rymaruk set down the last garbage can, crossed his arms and winked our way. I ignored him but Judy giggled and waved. "Look at those muscles! He's kind of cute."

"If you like that type," said Amy. "I don't."

I sat beside her on the stoop, glad that we had this in common. "Jews don't rot in hell," I pointed out. "We don't believe in miracles. We don't believe in idols or saints."

"That's true," said Amy thoughtfully.

Heartened, I offered slices of rye bread all around. While we chewed companionably I added, "Anyway, the floozy could be a very nice person."

The Widower Visarrion

That marital problems were not caused by outsiders, that outsiders could do nothing worse than people could do to themselves, was something my mother had shouted the night of the blizzard, when my father finally came home and she ran upstairs to their bedroom. I had recognized the comment as bizarre the moment she said it. And later, I would wonder again and again whatever possessed me to repeat it.

But that was later. Now, Amy's eyes narrowed.

"Of course, not as nice as Hannah's real mother," I added as she hooted and hooked arms with the others.

"I *hope* she's not as nice as Hannah's mother," Amy called back as they disappeared into her house. "And *my* mother says you shouldn't use their names in the same breath."

The next morning, Hannah stood in our doorway, one knee sock sagged to her ankle.

"Good morning, dear," my mother told her. "How pretty you look today. That color is very flattering with your hair and eyes."

Hannah's mother was working now, the only mother on Keer Avenue who had to, and mine had volunteered to keep an eye on Hannah in the afternoons until Mrs. Grabelsky got home. "She tells me you're doing very well in school," my mother said.

"I-I'm trying, Mrs. Tarlow. Arithmetic is hard. My f-f-father used to help me. He's very good at numbers."

My mother ran her hand over Hannah's brow, tucking stray hairs into her braids, which were always too loose now that Mrs. Grabelsky had to work. Out the window, I watched Judy Bluestone knock on Joyce Shapiro's door. When Joyce came out, they linked arms and walked the three houses to knock on Amy Siegel's.

"Your mother says that you wrote a beautiful essay on world peace," my mother told Hannah. "She's very proud of you. I'm sure your father is, too."

I turned and stared. How could she mention his name, and like that, without a trace of horror or disgust?

"I'll pick you both up after school today," she was telling Hannah. "We'll drive out to Short Hills. Mr. Tarlow and I found another house we like a lot. Marlene loves it but we'd like to get Debbie's opinion."

They had all gone to see it that Sunday, when I claimed a stomach ache and insisted on being dropped off at my grandmother's. There I spent a very pleasant afternoon helping bake rice pudding, several bowls of which I managed to get down.

"I think the house is fine," I said. "Go ahead and buy it. I'm sure it's the greatest house in the universe."

"My m-mother says Sh-Short Hills is b-beautiful. She says all the h-houses have huge lawns and that it's like another w-w-world."

I poured my cereal into the sink, let the bowl clatter, and gathered my things.

"It's like Uranus," I told Hannah, with the emphasis on the middle syllable.

She turned red and went for her coat. "Wait up," she was calling. "D-D-Debbie, wait up. I'm coming."

But her treacherous remark of support for my mother convinced me I now owed her nothing. I stormed out and only looked back when I was well up Keer Avenue and nearly had reached Amy Siegel and her friends. It wasn't my fault Mrs. Rymaruk had died. It wasn't my fault we were moving to Short Hills. It wasn't my fault poor Hannah walked so slowly.

According to my mother, it was. I heard the sound of her car before I saw it. She pulled alongside me, rolled down her window and motioned me over. I went to the curb, looking straight over her head at the house across the street.

"Look at me when I'm speaking to you," my mother said. "Don't pretend that you don't hear me."

Amy and the others now were far ahead, crossing to Bergen Street. Hannah was shuffling by with her eyes to the sidewalk, pretending not to notice my public shame. I kept my own eyes aimed past my mother, the rest of Keer Avenue in the periphery of my vision.

On one side, I saw Mrs. Siegel come out of her house and spend too much time plucking the newspaper from her front steps. On the other, I saw Mr. Rymaruk trudging to the bus stop.

"There's your friend," I said.

My mother glanced at Mrs. Siegel and frowned, shaking her head.

"I tolerate Estelle Siegel because I have to. And Amy is just like her. You know, Hannah has it very hard," said my mother. "I won't have you behaving this way. Think how you'd feel in her position."

"I didn't mean Mrs. Siegel."

A speck of dust on the windshield caught my mother's attention and, slowly, she wiped it away with the side of her hand. I kept staring at the house across the street and she stared at the windshield. Then she rolled down her window the last several inches, leaned past me, and waved.

When Mr. Rymaruk came to the car, she reached over and opened his door. He was wearing blue overalls and an unzipped brown parka. My father, even in work clothes, never looked as plain and faded.

"I'm going downtown," she told him. "I'll drop you. Step away from the curb," she warned without looking at me.

I moved an inch. She pulled into the Siegels' driveway, backed up, and drove off in the opposite direction.

When her car was nearly at the corner, I ran into the middle of Keer Avenue and hollered.

"Think how you'd feel in Mrs. Grabelsky's position. Bet you can't, either!"

But it was too late. They were gone. Only Hannah Grabelsky, waiting at the corner, saw me. She'd seen everything.

I spent the school day hoping for something practical to happen, like maybe my mother would get a flat tire or run out of gas. But at 3:15 her car was idling just beyond the playground. And poor little Hannah was sprawled in the back seat by the time I got there. My mother was laughing at something Hannah had said; I got in feeling silly and left out, and slammed the door as hard as I could.

My mother drove across Bergen Street and turned up South Orange Avenue, chatting about the house we were going to see.

"I hope you'll keep an open mind, because I brought a check. You have to look past the furnishings, of course—the carpets and wallpaper, things like that. The basement is finished in knotty pine and your father could have an office there. You and your sister could have a playroom and I could have a sewing room. It's exactly the house I've been searching for."

"Pop doesn't need an office. He never had one before and he doesn't need one now. We're too old for a playroom."

"This one might change your mind. We'd put a television down there, and the hi-fi. You'd have real privacy when your new friends came over. How was school?"

"I'm not making new friends. And I don't need privacy. I have nothing to hide."

By then, we had left Newark and were headed up a hill on which the houses had grown further and further apart. Gaining altitude, South Orange Avenue also had changed character. It was different here, quiet and lacking sidewalks or shops, hushed as our synagogue in the middle of the week. Further up, the hill became a mountain and the Reservation started, a kind of public park where my parents often took us to feed the deer on Sundays, when the law forbade my father's tavern to be open.

My mother kept silent as she turned left, right, down a winding lane alongside a pond. After several minutes we pulled up to a brick house with a carved eagle on the door. There was a mailbox shaped like a bird at the front of the drive, a girl's bicycle propped against the part that said, 'The Griffiths.' Another car was parked at the curb just ahead of us.

A woman my mother introduced as Mrs. Lyman got out and came over, smelling deliciously of perfume.

"So this is Debbie." I liked her right away because she didn't get me mixed up with Hannah. "It's very nice to meet you, Debbie."

"And this is Debbie's friend, Hannah," said my mother.

"'Hannah.' What an unusual and lovely name."

"It's Hannah Grabelsky," I told the realtor. "We have another one on our block, Hannah Morgenstern, but she's two years behind. She's only one year younger but she was held back in third grade."

Mrs. Lyman peered over her glasses at my mother, who was gazing at the house, her golden hair in a French twist and her hands folded in front of her. When Mrs. Lyman turned back to me, I thought I could tell what she was thinking.

"I don't really look like my parents," I volunteered. "Well, I kind of look like my father, but really I look exactly like my grandmother, Leah Edelman. We're dark. Everyone calls me her spitting image."

"Ah," she said. Then she nodded and led us up the walk.

Inside, Mrs. Griffith talked to my mother about which fixtures would stay and which would go if we bought the house, about which school was closest, and about real-estate taxes. After a while, she turned to me and Hannah. "Feel free to scout around, girls. My daughter Annie is in her room with some friends. She's about your age."

Upstairs, the rooms were arranged around a hallway wider than our living room. The door to the far bedroom was open. Just as my mother had hinted, everything inside it was a shade of pink and a manner of decoration that I despised—the lacy curtains, the flowered bedspread, even the fixture that hung from the ceiling, dangling small porcelain rosebuds.

Two girls sat cross-legged on the pink carpet and the third sat on the bed. That one looked up and smiled. "I'm Annie. Are you the girls who might move in here?"

I went to the window and looked down at the backyard. My mother was out there with Mrs. Lyman and Mrs. Griffith, admiring the shrubbery and the ceramic pots of plants along the patio.

"I am. I'm Debbie," I said.

At the bedroom door, Hannah had stayed standing. "She's my neighbor," I added. "On Keer Avenue."

"That's a pretty sweater," the one with bangs told her. "Is it mohair? I'm Heidi. Where's Keer Avenue?"

"In Newark," I said. "Down South Orange Avenue."

"My f-father is m-moving to Philadelphia," Hannah said suddenly. "He j-just got a job there."

"When are you moving?" asked Annie.

"I'm not m-m-moving. My f-father is. My mother and sisters and I are staying in Newark."

Heidi nodded. "My parents are divorced, too. My brother used to wake up crying every morning. But now he's fine."

"My parents aren't d-d-divorced. They're s-s-separated."

"That's the same thing," I said, and turned my back against all of them. Down in the yard, my mother had walked alone to the picket fence, where several elms and sycamores formed a small grove. The other two women stayed on the patio. Mrs. Lyman leaned toward Mrs. Griffith, who twisted the toe of her shoe on the edge of the slate and glanced up at the window. Short Hills, I thought, as she stared at my face. What a stupid name for a town. All hills were short, like all mountains were tall. Like all pizzas were pies, like all floozies were gentile. People here spoke about divorce as if it were normal. On Keer Avenue, only death was equal to a family's splitting apart.

Hannah walked across the pink carpet and tapped my shoulder.

"It's not the same thing," she told me, without a trace of her stutter. "It's not the same thing at all."

My mother drove back from Short Hills down South Orange Avenue. At the Jewish cemetery, we crossed the Newark city line. "So? What did you think?"

"It's fine," I said. "Did you give them the check?"

"I did." At the next traffic light, she reached back to pat my knee. "How did those other girls strike you?"

"They liked Hannah a lot."

My mother laughed. "What's not to like?"

"They liked Debbie too," Hannah said.

"You see? New things aren't so frightening when you give them a chance."

On Keer Avenue, we walked Hannah home. Dusk had fallen and her house was dark, but one by one the lights came on as we neared her front door. When Mrs. Grabelsky opened it, I expected to see John or Gregory Rymaruk in the living room. But instead, it was Mr. Rymaruk himself who was standing behind her, flicking the switches for the Sabbath.

There seemed to be nothing unusual about the way that he and my mother spoke to each other, just the typical grown-up complaints. Still, I watched them.

"John's off at a church retreat," said Mr. Rymaruk. "Gregory has some sort of sports dinner. They grow up way too fast. They stop for nothing."

My mother smiled. "Better that they don't," she told him, and Mr. Rymaruk sighed. He and Mrs. Grabelsky congratulated us on the house in Short Hills but my mother didn't make a big thing of it. She said she would rather hear about bookkeeping, which was what Mrs. Grabelsky did in her new job, so the three of them talked about that for a while. As we were leaving, I said I'd see Hannah on Monday morning, but she told me I ought to walk ahead to school with Amy Siegel.

Later that night, Marlene and my father wanted to know what I thought of the house, but by then I was tired and didn't feel like talking. I had changed into my pajamas without being told when the telephone rang. My father took it by his bed while my mother undid my pony tail and brushed out the knots.

"Mrs. Lyman, good to hear from you." He frowned and the vein on his forehead started to pulse. My mother laid the brush in her lap and put her hands on my shoulders.

"I don't understand. That check is good." In a few seconds he added, "No, we wouldn't be happier in Springfield or Livingston." Then his voice got low and even. "Oh, I think I understand you quite correctly. But let me tell you something, Mrs. Lyman. I work hard for a living. My wife tells me that I work *too* hard. In fact, we've had a few words on that subject—maybe that surprises you. This is the United States of America, Mrs. Lyman. My family has every right to live in Short Hills. Don't tell me what I think you're saying."

He hung up and sat on the edge of the bed with his big head bent into his hands. With a jolt, I noticed that he was beginning to bald. On his crown, a circle of flesh the size of a silver dollar caught the overhead light and gleamed faintly; it hadn't been there when the winter started.

"They returned the check," my mother said. "Am I right?"

"All of a sudden, the Griffiths don't want to sell. All of a sudden, they've decided to hold onto the house for a while."

For the first time that season, my heart surged with the old love I had felt for my parents, before all the talk of Short Hills had ruined the winter. And something else passed through me as I kissed them good-night, a feeling I had thought that only gentiles courted: for-giveness. But the moment I left them and got into bed, I started to shudder, the way that I always shuddered after crossing myself in the girls' bathroom at school, to see if I could trick the God of the gentiles, who took complaints more often than ours, into making things turn out the way I wanted. Because landscaped Tudor or up-to-date split level, frame colonial or pristine ranch: to me, every possibility had seemed certain exile, with only a miracle to prevent it from happening. And on Keer Avenue none of us, except of course for Mr. Rymaruk, believed in that sort of thing.

But if this was a miracle, it turned out to be granted in error. Although my parents gave up house-hunting for the next several years, eventually they found another realtor. They made an offer on a center-hall colonial that cost more than the first house; without any haggling, their offer was accepted and all the papers signed. We moved a few months later. By that time, most everyone else on Keer Avenue was moving, too.

Yet, after all of that, my mother still drove down South Orange Avenue to Bergen Street to buy our meat and poultry at Dumbroff's, until the shop closed and moved to Livingston. For a few years, my father still drove up South Orange Avenue to get home from his tavern. They both joined the PTA at my school, and for a while, my mother led my Girl Scout troop. Otherwise, my parents didn't have much to do with the new neighbors. They kept to themselves.

Perhaps, when I stood shaking with shame in the bathroom at school, the God of the gentiles had glanced down and recognized me for who I was, just as clearly as had Mrs. Griffith when she stood in her landscaped backyard, staring up at my Jewish face in her daughter's window.

We keep in our hearts, or under our tongues like tablets of nitro-glycerine, whole worlds that have exploded. A few years ago, many years after we all moved away from New Jersey, my sister and I brought our kids to visit my mother in Florida. One afternoon we took them to Sea World, where we ran into Mr. Rymaruk and his younger son, Gregory. Mr. Rymaruk now lived alone in Boca Raton, in a low-rise overlooking a golf course. Gregory was visiting from California, where he produced some sort of high-brow videos and movies, or at least that was his claim. In truth, Gregory had struck me as a possible pornographer ever since the day he winked at Amy Siegel and the rest of us, although, later, when I mentioned this to Marlene, she laughed and said that I'd always had a dangerous imagination. Evidently John was on his third wife. He had become a lawyer, not a priest.

On a crowded walkway near the seal pond, my mother and Mr. Rymaruk talked about the families we had known on Keer Avenue, about which particular disease had taken each of the men, and about which of the widows lived in which Florida town. Excepting, as always, Mr. Rymaruk, not a single father still survived, and this felt sad but right to me, the way that things were meant to end.

They talked about the Cubans who were moving up from South Miami all across south Florida. Mr. Rymaruk said he had no intention of learning Spanish at his age, and my mother said she worried that, next thing, the rednecks who loved David Duke would rise up against the Jews. And then, with her back already to the sea, where would she go?

I was surprised, and embarrassed, at her vehemence on the subject. But Mr. Rymaruk nodded in agreement.

"These days you've got to be careful where you settle. You never know who you'll wind up living next to," he said.

The salt breeze raised the hairs surviving on his head, then laid them gently down. Reaching out, he took my mother's hand. It was the hand that she had mangled many years ago, in a household accident. Now the last two fingers ended at the joints. But Mr. Rymaruk didn't seem bothered. He bent forward, lifted her hand, and pressed his lips to her palm.

"I always had this crazy wish that those stumps would grow back," she said.

"You always were a looker," Mr. Rymaruk told her. "Victor was one lucky guy."

My mother's smile still was beautiful, lighting up her celery eyes. Along with the inevitable slashes of white, her hair still had a trace of blonde in it.

"'Luck'? Vic never banked on that," she laughed. "Work was where he put his hope. But you, Visarrion, always were a charmer."

Until that moment, I had never realized that he had an actual first name. It didn't surprise me, though, to discover that the name was one I couldn't have guessed. *The Widower Visarrion*. I liked the drama of it.

But he never had remarried, and so I told my mother that the sun might make the kids dehydrated if we stayed much longer.

"You're unbelievable," my sister whispered as we turned to go.

She drove us back to the oceanside complex where my mother lived, following the Intracoastal past high-rises white and unreal as ghost towns made of bone. My mother sat in the front passenger seat and I sat in back with the kids. Over their laughter and singing, the three of us began to reminisce about the years we lived in Newark—about Hannah Grabelsky, the Eisenbergs, the Siegels, and the others. My mother's memories were fond. When I asked her, in a tone I hoped was neutral, why, then, had we moved away, she shrugged and listed the usual reasons.

"First, the schools. And the convenience, the beauty, the safety. Plus, your father appreciated the low real-estate taxes, Short Hills being such an old and established town. We were upwardly mobile. In those days, everyone was."

I didn't know what to say to this, since her reasons were so clear and obvious—documented in every study of urban demise I'd ever read. Yet I couldn't let the subject go.

"Still and all," I pointed out. "We could have moved to Springfield or Livingston or even West Orange."

We had arrived at the condominium complex. The kids were heading to the pool, stripping their shirts and shorts as they ran to jump in the water. Marlene's youngest bounced at the end of the diving board, calling for our attention. My mother held up her palm to me, the one whose poor stumps Mr. Rymaruk had blessed with his kiss. "Hold on a minute," she said, and walked to the edge of the pool to cheer on the next generation's Mark Spitz, her own true flesh and blood.

I got out of the car and leaned against the hood. When she came back, I repeated my question.

She slid her sunglasses onto her forehead and fisted her hands on her hips, staring at me in a sort of heated surprise, as if too much sun had blurred *my* senses: something so obvious, yet I hadn't seen it. All those years looking, and I hadn't seen it.

"I didn't want you and your sister to grow up believing that every gentile was a floozy. Or a murderer of Jews. I felt very strongly about that. So did your father," my widowed mother told me. "Especially your father."

I could see by her expression that she was thinking of him, and those years she spent too many nights alone. And so I turned from her, toward the ocean, and watched a gang of seagulls dart along the sand, scavenging the day's remains. The waves gleamed in the sunset and cracked close along the shore, as the last old people gathered up their things to leave. I watched them shrug their fragile and diminished limbs into cover-ups that seemed too loose, and I thought then that I should take my children to see Newark. I had often meant to do that. But with no one there for us to visit, I always told myself they would grow bored, that they would grow impatient, that they would wonder what it was I meant to say, and why I couldn't just say it. I always told myself they wouldn't recognize the ghostly sites to which I'd point, the vanished places that I would want to show them.

Dusk had nearly fallen. My heart was beating much too quickly. I turned back from the sea to watch the faded beauty in my mother's face. I realized then that I had never seen the phantom pain of the man she called "Visarrion." I had never seen hers either, nor that the rest of us were always bound, in time, to share it.

KEER AVENUE,
JULY 1967

It was so hot that Larry Eisenberg and I agreed to time how long an ice cube would take to melt on the hood of his mother's Pontiac. Larry had wanted to fry eggs on the sidewalk, but his mother wouldn't give us any, and no one in my family could agree on how they liked their eggs cooked, so my mother wouldn't buy them. Larry held my father's watch, a Timex Pop no longer wore, and I said "Go" and "Stop." In less than a minute, a puddle formed on the burning metal. In less than another minute, the water was gone.

That's how hot it was when Marlene came walking up Keer Avenue with Larry's sister, Paula. Actually, they weren't really walking—more like sashaying from one tree to the next, talking about boys they'd like to date and colleges they'd eventually like to go to. The hair near their ears was taped into spit-curls. Each of them wore the top of a two-piece bathing suit. Over the bottoms of the suits, they wore pleated *skorts*.

Skorts were skirts the length of shorts, and all the rage that summer. My mother had bought me one similar to Marlene's, but it was stuffed in a corner of my closet. My father hated two-piece bathing suits, and he hated skorts, because they were so short he thought any wily boy could see clear to Marlene's "kishkes." But that morning, he had let her wear one. That's how hot it was.

My mother wasn't home yet. The note she had left on the kitchen table, telling us to take some lemonade and eat the left-over chicken if she was late, had faded from heat by the time the bus dropped me off after day camp. All of the campers knew that our driver suffered from what he called "wife troubles," and evidently, in the heat, his troubles had flared up. As we rode along, he kept jerking the door opened and closed while the bus was moving. *Whack-whack* was the sound the door made. He had peeled off his shirt and the hair on his chest and his arms glimmered with sweat.

"I ask her what she wants, but do I get an answer? I get no answer. She takes her own sweet time," our driver kept saying.

Whack-whack.

We could have been killed. One after the other, each of us could have rolled off that bus and splattered the street. A layer of dead Jewish Nu-Teens would coat the hot asphalt.

"Did I ask her such a difficult question? Something so impossible to answer?"

We were talking as loud as we could, but all of us heard it.

"No, I did not," our driver told himself. "She knows the answer, but why should she say? Once she says, then it's all over."

The air in the bus was as hot as a pizza oven by the time we had driven down the Watchung Mountains and into dried yellow farmland, through towns with only one or two stores, and then past new suburbs of look-alike split-levels. As we crossed back into Newark, everyone started to stand. I thought the backs of my legs would peel off, but only two ovals of sweat stayed on the seats. Standing while the bus moved was against the rules, but that day we all rolled from the front to the back of the bus or pretended to, while our driver banged the door opened and closed.

Whack-whack. Whack-whack.

Larry and I had been out by the curb in front of his house for an hour or so by the time Marlene and Paula spread long sheets of aluminum foil on the brown grass and collapsed on their backs, their belly-buttons aimed at the sky as they worked at their tans, blabbing away about the Salzman twins who lived on the corner. Both of their faces were starting to peel. A red patch of raw skin had shredded a hole in Paula's forehead.

Marlene wanted Billy and Paula wanted Stewart. Larry rolled his eyes. "What difference does it make which one you get?" he asked. "They're twins."

He handed me the Timex and plopped an ice cube on his sister's stomach. Paula yelped and tossed it back at him, and Mrs. Eisenberg came out fanning herself with a *TV Guide.*

"Thirty seconds," she called to Larry and Paula. "That's how long you've got to get in here for supper."

Larry shrugged and slid the last ice cube onto the Pontiac's hood. It sizzled and in less than thirty seconds was gone. "I don't feel like eating," he told her.

Larry didn't go to day camp. In April, after his mother had paid the deposit and couldn't get it back, he announced that she could yell all she wanted, but he wasn't getting on a bus every morning to go play newcomb and make trivets out of Popsicle sticks in the Watchung mountains with a bunch of kids he hardly knew. After three days of fighting, his mother said fine, if that was how he wanted things. Now Larry was sorry, because every weekday morning he was tutored in the several subjects he had flunked that spring. In the afternoons his mother let him do whatever he wanted, but what he wanted was to ride his new bike and he had no one good to ride with. During the school year, we generally ignored each other, but every afternoon that summer, Larry pretended he just happened to be on the corner at 4:30 when the bus dropped me off. Except for this, I couldn't detect any real improvement in him. But it was nice to see a familiar face waiting, so I always let him take my camp bag and ride alongside me while I walked up Keer Avenue.

"Fruit salad and cold borscht," Mrs. Eisenberg said, on her way back in. "You have to put something in your stomach. In this weather, you'll get sick on an empty stomach."

Larry said he'd see me later, after he ate his fruit salad. He said Mrs. Eisenberg didn't really care if he had the borscht, she just served it every so often to make some kind of point. "My father hates it too. My mother says I'm just like him and she doesn't know why she wastes her time trying to get me to be different. Who am I supposed to be like, anyway? That's what my father always says. 'Who should he be like, Evelyn, the milkman?'" But when he and Paula dragged themselves into their house, Marlene said we'd better go in, too, and set the table.

As soon as we started, the telephone rang and she pulled the cord into the bathroom to take it. When she shut the door, I ran upstairs to my parents' room. It took her about five seconds to realize I was on the line.

"Deborah Ann, get off the phone," she yelled.

I put my hand over the receiver and stayed on. In another five seconds, Marlene rushed in.

I leaned against the headboard and took a copy of *Life* from the night table, acting as if I didn't hear a word of her screaming. The magazine cover was a color photograph of Moshe Dayan in khakis, a black patch on one eye. Behind him, young Israeli soldiers waved their fists from the tops of armored tanks. Inside was a picture of more soldiers praying at the Wailing Wall.

Marlene grabbed the magazine and stood there glowering. I closed my eyes and pretended to sleep. "Oooh," I said, while drifting off. "I can't stay awake in this weather."

For over a year, Marlene had been shaving her legs, locking herself in the bathroom and taking forever, never cleaning the little black hairs out of the tub. I moaned sleepily as I turned onto my side and peered at her thighs. They were tan and creamy-smooth, and you couldn't tell by looking that a single hair ever had a home there. What did she do, shave all the way up past the hem of her skort—straight to those dangerous kishkes?

I followed her toward the stairs as she angrily called for my mother again and again, as if I'd been lying about the note, or Mama was hiding. But, luckiest of days, my mother wasn't back yet.

Marlene and I held out against hunger as long as we could. We were sitting at the kitchen table, starting on the leftover roast chicken, when she walked in. It was long past suppertime, even past the time when my father usually came home. Marlene still wouldn't speak to me, but without a word of discussion, we had wheeled in the television set. As soon as we heard the keys in the door, we threw down our drumsticks and began wheeling the TV back into the den.

My mother walked past us. Her blonde hair was pinned up, but half of it was hanging in her eyes. She went straight to the refrigerator and pulled a pitcher of iced tea onto the counter. Her hand shook as she poured the tea into a glass filled with ice cubes. She didn't mention the TV. That's how hot it was.

"I'm sorry I'm late." She glanced at our plates and added, "I'm glad you girls have gone ahead with dinner."

Right away, Marlene started tattling. "She's a baby and a brat. I have zero privacy, none at all, I can't even have a simple phone conversation without hearing her snoopy little breath on the other end."

The windows were open, but the kitchen was filled with prickly humidity. My mother was flushed and her blouse was sweat-stained. She leaned over and angled the table fan at her face, but Marlene snapped it off.

My mother's hair stopped blowing. "Sweetie, what are you doing?"

Marlene folded her arms and bit her lip. "I was telling you something and you weren't listening."

On her bottom lip, Marlene was getting a fever blister, a natural disaster that always drove her wild. I leaned over and whispered.

"Bite a little harder until it blows up like a salami, and Billy Salzman won't go near you with a ten-foot pole."

"Mama! Listen to her!"

"I'm sorry. I'm beat. I had to go down to your father's tavern and see how he was." My mother's eyes were closed, but the pair behind her head was working as she got up and went to the refrigerator. "Deborah Ann, don't push your luck."

Then she opened the freezer door and pulled out a clear plastic bag of sheets and clothes, pre-sprinkled and set to chill so they'd iron out fresh—the sleeves on my father's white work shirts grabbing her blouses, my camp shorts kneeing a few of Marlene's pleated skorts. My mother set the bundle on the counter and stuck her head next to a half-gallon of ice cream. It was so hot in the kitchen that the frosty clothes immediately began melting. By the time she cooled down and turned back to us, a few sleeves hung limp from the counter. The whole bundle was flattening, and water dripped to the floor.

"They're rioting downtown," my mother said. "On South Orange Avenue, across Broad Street, clear to Central Avenue. Your father and Sherman and a few of his other men are standing guard outside his tavern. Your father has his billyclub, but so far, he hasn't had to use it."

Pop kept his billyclub in his night table, sometimes in the glove compartment of his car, sometimes at his tavern—depending where he was. The billyclub was thicker than the circle I could make between my thumb and index finger. It possessed a surprising elasticity. If you gripped the end and whacked, the tip would swing out first.

"Thank God none of them has a gun." My mother held the half-gallon of ice cream under her chin and moved it around to the back of her neck as she kept talking. "Moe Kaminsky had one and managed to put a bullet in his foot. We saw flames down South Orange Avenue, but—thank God—the fire didn't get up to us. I saw an old woman walking down South Orange Avenue in a full-length mink from Fatell's, the furrier. Can you imagine? In this heat? Your uncles' grocery store was burned to the ground. Look," she said, and pointed out the window.

Her car was in the driveway, its front end crinkled in like a piece of aluminum foil. The grille was stuffed with long yellow and black splinters of wood.

"There were police barricades all around the Central Ward. That engine has a lot of power, though," my mother said. "I hardly felt the impact."

I gasped and she dropped the half-gallon of ice cream on the linoleum. Marlene stood straight up and knocked over her chair. Then my mother stepped forward and pulled us both close. The three of us stood that way a while, with her face pressed against a cheek of each of ours. I looked out at our driveway, at the smashed fender of her car, and at Keer Avenue, graying as the sun went down. I tried to imagine the Central Ward in flames: Broad & Market, South Orange Avenue, Springfield Avenue, Halsey Street, High Street, Branford Place, all of it. My mother had said that the city was burning, but I only had her word for it. I only had her version. In front of my own two eyes was nothing unusual—just the steamy haze of summer evening, and a few lightning bugs that flickered near the maple tree out back, by my rusting swing set.

Then something rustled in the azalea bushes, and all three of us jumped. Two houses down, a pair of cats dashed across the lawn toward the bowl of water that Mr. Rymaruk always left on his back stoop. Larry was out there, waving his arms for me, so eventually I grabbed an empty jar from the pantry and a Milky Way from the freezer and went outside to join him.

To avoid scaring off the lightning bugs, Larry and I never talked at the start of our hunts. In silence, we crept toward the trees and bushes that divided the yards, holding out our jars. When a lightning bug flew near, we scooped it in. Earlier in the summer, my father had punched air holes in the lids, so the bugs could breathe but not escape. If we wanted to capture them, he said, then we should be humane about it. We shouldn't rob them of their oxygen, since we didn't intend to kill the bugs, just to take their light. "Get enough of these and we'll save a fortune on electricity," he told us on evenings when Larry and I did exceptionally well.

My mother was safe, but he still wasn't home. I held out my jar and tried to imagine how hot he must be, standing outside his tavern with Sherman Carter, watching the flames eat downtown while his customers went shopping in the ruins. I didn't understand why he needed a billyclub to fight fire, or why he thought he could stop it from burning his tavern by pacing on the sidewalk with Sherman and the rest of his men. For a split second, I saw his big, burly body whirl to the sky in a flash of orange and red.

Then I couldn't breathe. But in another second, my lungs opened up, and I saw Larry, lilac bushes, and lightning bugs.

"Did your mother tell you?" I asked him.

Larry had disappeared into the darkness and I was speaking to a clump of lilacs. "She's upstairs with a headache," he called back. "Tell me what?"

When Larry crawled out, dried-out lilacs clung to his hair and his neck. But although it had grown dark, I could see him perfectly, because all around the neighborhood, people's televisions were on. And on every screen, a newscaster was speaking into a microphone against a background of bluish gray flames.

"Well, there are riots downtown tonight," I told him.

"I hope they end soon. All these TVs are making the lightning bugs think it's not dark enough to show what they can do."

I reached out and unscrewed the lid on his jar. The bugs flew away and disappeared into the bushes, taking their small lanterns with them. Larry's face crumpled in as if I'd just smacked it with my father's billyclub.

"Tonight my uncles' grocery store was burned to the ground. Do you think you'll be able to ride your stupid bike around Newark all day long if your father's hardware store burns down, too? Didn't your mother tell you what a riot was?"

Larry dropped his empty jar and it rolled along the grass. "She said something crazy was happening downtown because of the heat."

"Didn't you ask what was so crazy?"

"I figured she meant that people were opening the fire hydrants so they'd have someplace to cool off. They do that every summer."

I took Larry's hand and led him to the street. His eyes were round now, and I could see that he wasn't a smart-alecky moron, only frightened. We went to the curb and I smacked the frozen Milky Way against the gutter. I gave Larry half so he'd calm down.

"It means real fire." I pointed in the direction of downtown. "She should have told you."

It always had amazed me that boys like Larry grew up to be fathers, but that night I surprised myself by feeling close to him, sitting on the curb and listening to the sounds of summer: the cats charging in and out of the azalea bushes, the Salzman twins slapping a handball against their garage door, the city bus rumbling along Weequahic Avenue, and from the opened windows of the houses on Keer Avenue, the wails of the younger kids arguing about bed-times and teeth-brushing. All the sounds were the same as usual, except for everybody's television sets turned up too high.

That night, our mothers forgot to call us in, and neither of us saw any point in reminding them. But finally, when we finished our Milky Ways and the sky was black, I watched Larry walk inside his house and flick on the outside light. Then I went inside my own house.

I found my mother in the kitchen hanging up the phone, and Marlene ready to kill me, because I had left her with the dishes. Mama had just talked to Pop.

"Your father won't be coming home tonight. Or if he does, it won't be until much later," she said, which meant the same thing since it was nearly time for Johnny Carson. She said Marlene could watch Johnny with her, but not me of course, because I had day camp in the morning. But the voice my mother used was different than her absolutely-not voice, and she was so mixed up that she went upstairs and laid down on my father's side of the bed instead of hers.

After I washed my face, I went in to kiss her good-night, ignoring Marlene, who was propped on pillows beside her as though she were a regular wife and Mama was her husband. The sight made me sick to my stomach, both of them with their ice-cream-smooth legs sticking out flat from their nighties like four matched Popsicle sticks. I didn't like the idea of trying to sleep without my father in the house, so after I had gone to my room, I crawled back out on my stomach and laid on the carpet at the foot of my parents' bed, trying not to breathe. On television, Johnny Carson was dressed up like a swami, squinting at a crystal ball.

I guess my mother didn't like the idea of sleeping without Pop either, because the TV was static by the time I closed my eyes. I could still hear their voices. Actually, what I thought I heard was Mama whisper, "Shh. Keep your voice low. She's right down there."

The next morning on her way to the bathroom to give herself a manicure, Marlene stepped on my hair accidentally on purpose, so right away the day started wrong.

My father still wasn't back.

That was the summer my mother could have written a book if she'd put together all the notes she left us. There was one on the carpet beside me when my eyes first felt the sun, reminding me to take my vitamins before leaving the house. There was another on the bathroom sink, banning the swimming pool for two hours after lunch, even if my counselor said okay. So after I dressed and went downstairs to the kitchen, it was Marlene pouring out my Frosted Flakes instead of my mother, and it was Marlene slicing the banana to float on top, and it was Marlene who made my lunch that day.

I took my seat at the table and watched her, trying to remember when she had learned to do everything she suddenly was doing. I pressed my spoon onto the Frosted Flakes and drowned them in the milk. After a while I said, "You don't have to bother with all that. I've decided not to go to camp today." Maybe I wouldn't even leave the house. Maybe I would straighten up my room. For weeks, my mother had been after me about it.

"You're being dramatic, a regular Sarah Heartburn," Marlene said without looking up. "And I'm not staying here all day with you. I promised Paula to go with her to Weequahic Park."

"Not today you shouldn't. Mama wouldn't let you."

"We talked about it while you were sleeping. She said it was okay as long as we head to the far end." That was where Newark stopped and the adjacent town of Hillside started.

"That's very big of you," I said. "Newark is in flames and Pop, or even Mama, could be lying somewhere in a pool of blood. But you and Paula will spend the afternoon working on your suntans."

"Paula's upset. Not that it's any of your business anyway."

"Everyone's upset."

She shrugged her shoulders, selecting peaches from the bowl on the counter. "So—that's why. Where's your lunch box?"

"In the pantry, where it always is."

"Do you want rye bread or challah?"

"I want pumpernickel."

"There's no pumpernickel."

"Who cares, then."

She held up my lunchbox and shook it. "You know something, Deborah Ann? This may surprise you. But I don't intend to do this all my life. I'm not like Mama. I'm going to travel. I'm going to see some places that are different than Bradley Beach or even Florida."

The *Newark News* lay open on the table. The top of the front page was filled with pictures of the Central Ward—firemen with their hoses aimed like rifles, policemen swinging truncheons, people running. Outside on Keer Avenue, the air was steaming up, or had stayed that way all night. The edges of everything seemed merged together, indistinct. The scene was no different than usual, the soft fine mesh of summer morning, open and inviting to whatever you wanted to make of it. One of Mr. Rymaruk's guest cats sat motionless on our lawn, like a statue of a cat. The other sprawled nearby on its belly.

I let my eyes move across the grass. My mother's car was gone from our driveway and in the street lay a long splinter of yellow wood that must have fallen from its grille when she left that morning.

On her toes, my sister was reaching to the highest cabinet. I thought she'd need the stepstool, but she yanked down the box of aluminum foil.

"Okay, rye bread," I told her.

"And we won't be working on our suntans."

"Then what's the foil for?"

"It's to wrap your sandwich in." She tore it off, the sound of slashing metal. "Satisfied?"

"Mama uses cellophane."

"It's called Saran Wrap, not cellophane. Cellophane is something else."

"She doesn't use aluminum foil. That's for hot stuff and a waste of money for a sandwich. Anyway, I hate the sound when I unwrap it."

"*Okay.*"

She slid the box of foil back into the cabinet and yanked down the box of Saran Wrap.

"So if you're not going to work on your tans, then what will you and Paula do at Weequahic Park?"

"Take a *walk. Talk*, okay?"

This was something new between us—the steady bicker which my mother hated, warning that we'd waste away our love and leave real scars if we weren't careful. But that morning, sparring with Marlene seemed a kind of comfort. I kept it up.

"I suppose the Salzman twins will hang around, too, to help you and Paula *walk.*"

"Don't just eat the Frosted Flakes and leave the milk. You always do that."

"The last flakes get soggy. They're disgusting when they're soggy."

"That's because you let them sit there."

"Why can't I stay home?"

"Because you should go to camp. The day will seem like a year if you hang around the house and watch the clock."

"Don't start," I told her. "I didn't laugh at your stupid spitcurls, so don't you laugh about Pop's Timex. It was Larry's idea, anyway."

"I only meant that it's going to be a long day for everybody and there's nothing we can do to speed it up." Marlene poured my thermos full of juice and sighed. "We'll just have to wait and see."

She sounded exactly like my mother then, mouthing Mama's words, mushing the mayonnaise into the tuna, cutting off the crusts of the rye bread, wrapping up cake for my lunchbox: almond eyes, cheekbone-girl, a stick figure in the process of adding dimension, with a few real curves and a Band-Aid just below the hem of her skort from shaving her legs. Being a woman was something like being a boss, but evidently different, too: similar, but not the same exactly. Something intangible but quite specific was involved.

As my sister moved fluidly from counter to refrigerator and back again, I could see it starting, not at all what I'd expected, or ever thought could really happen. It felt like a surprise attack.

"You know, if a girl goes on dates or even has a boyfriend, it doesn't mean she changes into some kind of foreigner," she told me a few minutes later. "It's not like that."

Marlene had walked me to the corner to await the bus for day camp and was braiding my hair with a rubberband in her mouth. The sun was a seething red globe low in the sky and old Mr. Weintraub, who crossed kids on their way to Weequahic Park, had tossed his jacket on the stop sign. Marlene's fingers smelled of tuna, and I hoped the flakes of fish on them would spoil in the heat when she went walking in the park with Paula.

I kept looking up and down Weequahic Avenue for either my mother's banged-up heap, or my father's convertible, but there weren't many cars out yet.

"Stop yanking. When Mama does my hair, I barely feel a thing. And you can't have a steady boyfriend. Pop says you're not old enough."

"I can have dates." Marlene's voice was mumbly because a third of my hair was tucked in her mouth. "I don't want a steady boy-friend anyway."

"Because you're too young," I said. "Too young for dates, too, according to Pop."

"Pop says a lot of things he knows can't happen. Like making you promise you'll never get your hair cut, even when you're married and have kids."

Marlene's hair was cut just above her ears, sliced in layers I con-sidered beautiful. For a long time, I'd been whining about wanting my own hair chopped just like it. All summer, I'd complained that my hair was too heavy and even in braids made me sweat in the heat.

"I'm not getting married. I'm not having kids. I might adopt one, but I'm not *hav*ing any. And you're pulling too hard," I told her. "You're hurting my head."

She lifted my hair and wiped the sweat from the back of my neck with the hem of her skort. "Squinch down."

"Anyway, some day Pop will let me cut my hair," I added. "He has to."

"Obviously," she said. "That's my point."

When the bus came, I traded a slice of cake for a window seat, thinking I might see my father gnawing a cigar as he drove along

Weequahic Avenue and turned up Keer. But I never saw his black convertible pass, and I didn't see my mother's car, either. Marlene had given me an an extra slice of cake, so on the way home from camp I traded for another window seat, but I didn't expect to see the convertible in mid-day, and I didn't. I didn't see anything else out of the ordinary for such a brutal summer, either, except that the Good Humor men were handing out extra napkins to the kids buying treats because their Popsicles were melting so fast.

In the morning, our driver sat silent and bare-chested at the wheel. But on the way home that afternoon, when we stopped for a light, a bus from a rival camp pulled up beside us. Right away, everyone rushed to one side to stick their heads out for a singing contest with the other campers and I regretted trading my second slice of cake, because I could have had my window seat for nothing.

While we waited for the light to change, the other driver yanked open his door.

Whack-whack.

"Hey Wilson, how's tricks?"

Even over all that singing, we could hear our driver hollering back about his wife.

"About as bad as they could be." He spread his fingers and rubbed his hand across his hairy chest, up to his throat. Pools of sweat had settled there. "Look at me. I haven't slept in days and she still takes her sweet time answering. Does she want me to stay? Does she want me to go?"

"Can't live *with* them, can't kill them," called the other driver.

"To get a cup of coffee in the morning, it's like asking for charity. To get dinner, or just some food in the refrigerator to heat up when I come home, that's like asking for charity. And forget the bedroom altogether. That's like asking a Jew for an interest-free loan."

"It's the heat," the other driver told him. "Even rabbits have to cool their jets in this damned heat. Myself, I haven't gotten any in over a month. I'm just trying to hang on until autumn."

"Autumn?" Our driver stared down at his gleaming chest, then out at the dense, unmoving air. "Autumn's never going to come to this city."

At the corner of Keer Avenue, Larry was waiting on his bike, as usual. On the way home, he said that he and Paula were eating supper at my house that night, because his mother was nervous about his father's store on Lyons Avenue, nearly in Irvington, and had gone up there to be with him. According to Larry, my mother had said she'd pick up some pizzas at Jo-Ray's on her way home from the Central Ward. He didn't seem to realize that having pizza for dinner instead of for snack meant that things must be bad at my father's tavern.

When Larry went in his house and came out with the tray of ice cubes, I said, "My father might get aggravated if he knew we were using his Timex to watch ice cubes melt."

"He said we could use that Timex whenever we wanted. Your mother gave him a new watch last Hanukah. Don't you remember?"

"Of course I remember. They're my parents, not yours."

"Look," Larry said. "Do you want to do the ice cubes, and I'll do the Timex?"

We finished off the tray, and it really was more satisfying to be the one watching the ice cubes instead of the little hand on the Timex, watching all those seconds that took forever to pass, and the hour hand that didn't seem ever to move. There was no comparison between being the one with the watch and being the one who handled the cubes, and I felt irritated with myself for having so often let Larry call the shots that summer.

A little later, Marlene and Paula showed up with an old beach blanket and a deck of playing cards. They asked if we felt like killing some time, so for a while the four of us sat on the lawn and played Go Fish. But when the Salzman twins turned the corner, my sister took the deck. Cross-legged on the blanket, she shuffled and re-shuffled with a gorgeous grace. She cupped her hands—diamonds, clubs, hearts and spades rose into a perfect bridge between them. When had she learned to do this? Larry and Paula were astonished as rubes.

By then the twins had reached us. Billy, the one my sister wanted, leaned down and squinted at her skill.

"That's pretty good," he said.

Marlene smiled and her bridge of cards collapsed into a pile.

"I can do that too," said Billy. He gathered up the cards and started shuffling, with bravado but no art. So I elbowed Larry, and we got up and went around to his backyard, where we took turns throwing pebbles to see how many dead roses we could knock off Mr. Rymaruk's dried-up bushes.

Marlene and Paula stayed the whole time on the front lawn, talking with the Salzman twins. The hot breeze drifted the playing cards, one by one, into the curb. No one noticed or went to pick them up.

Around dusk, my mother came home with the pizzas, which were luke-warm and not nearly as good as usual. After we finished eating, she told us we could clean up later, which I'd never heard her say before. So we all went outside to wait, pressing against our foreheads the damp cloths in which she had wrapped frozen cans of Scotch Ice. Lots of people did the same thing that night as they walked up and down Keer Avenue, gathered in threes and fours on the parched lawns, listening to transistor radios and swatting at mosquitoes. Larry and I each had a flashlight, and for a while we went around shining them at the sky or holding them in front of people's faces, pretending we were TV reporters. When Mr. and Mrs. Eisenberg came home, they didn't have much to say, so eventually we went and joined some other kids who were playing Statues on the Rymaruks' lawn. One kid would grab your wrist and swing you around and around in a circle until you got dizzy, and then the kid would let go and you'd stagger onto the grass and freeze into place, your arms and legs twisted in strange positions. And you would hold that position as long as you could, not only pretending, but actually believing, that by nothing more powerful than an act of will, you could command the muscles of your body to transcend time and place and turn different, elsewhere, fixed and safe.

Those moments when we scattered across the lawns, onto the sidewalks and along the curbs, seemed to last and last. We were a garden of human statuary refusing to move from Keer Avenue. Only our breathing, the rise and fall of our lungs, gave us away.

I was a few lawns down, trying to balance with one leg behind me, when my father's black convertible turned the corner and came slowly up Keer Avenue. He pulled all the way into our driveway, shut off the ignition and got out of the car. One of the boys had grabbed Larry's hand and was whirling him around. They let go of each other, and Larry made a show of stumbling across the Rymaruks' lawn. Then he froze in place on the end of my driveway, just behind my father's car. Larry contorted himself and was facing the street, as usual not paying attention. All of the grown-ups froze in place, as if they too were playing Statues, and watched the convertible roll toward Larry. At the bump in the driveway the car rolled up, *whack,* it rolled up and, just before it came down, my father realized what was happening. He ran back to the car, jumped into the driver's seat, and jammed on the emergency brake.

At that point, everyone started moving and talking. The women began fanning themselves with rolled-up newspapers; the men shook their heads and wiped their faces on their shirtsleeves. Pop looked relieved when he spotted Marlene, who had wandered with Billy Salzman to the dark side of our house, but he didn't say a word about her skort. It was still that hot.

He seemed okay when I ran over and shined the flashlight up and down his body. His arms were streaked with soot and he walked without his usual energy, but he wasn't burned or beaten.

In fact, he had unwrapped a cigar, and after we kissed, I said, "Are you hungry? There's pizza."

"Oh, no. Sherman's wife brought us a huge plate of ham hocks and we ate them all through the night and into the day. I'm stuffed. Betty is a wonderful cook."

"You ate that? No kidding."

"It's like bacon, but better."

"Do the riots mean we're going to be poor now?" I said.

"Oh no, Sweetie, of course not."

"So I won't have to drop out of day camp? Marlene can go to college if she wants?"

My father snapped his lighter at the cigar, and the hot air smelled like a man. "People will be drinking liquor even more now. Mark my words."

"What about Heshie and Lou?" I asked.

"Well—your uncles will be out of work for a while, that's for sure. Their place took a beating."

"Can't you loan them some money?"

"Sure I can, Sweetie. Don't worry."

"Will you give them an interest-free loan?"

He frowned and stared. "'Interest-free?' Where'd you hear a phrase like that?"

"Will you?"

"No, Deborah, I won't. I'll be giving them the money, free and clear. Or, more probably, your Uncle Nat will. Does that meet with your approval?"

"Why was their grocery store burned to the ground?"

He glanced around for my mother, but she was one house over, talking to Mr. Rymaruk. I stepped in front of my father so he couldn't get away. Standing that close, I could smell the ashes in his hair.

"When you're older, you'll understand," he told me.

But people were always telling me that, and I had grown tired of hearing it. "That's not an answer," I said.

"I don't *have* the answer, Sweetheart. I'm just one working man and I can only tell you what I saw and what I think. What I saw were riots. What I think is that nothing makes sense when people riot." He sighed, and stared in the direction of the Central Ward. In a quieter voice, he added, "Why they riot, or why they didn't riot sooner."

"But your tavern wasn't burned. So why was the uncles' grocery store?"

"I need a bath," he said, still staring toward the Central Ward. "I'm hot as hell."

Sometimes, when you have finally stopped thinking that you can get people to tell you what they've planned not to give up, they say things that surprise you. My father's next words did that.

"These things don't just happen, Sweetheart. Nothing in life just happens. Heshie and Jake stole from their customers for many years," my father told me. "Everybody down there knew it. That's all I can tell you."

Finally, the air grew somewhat cooler. I left my father and went over to the row of azalea bushes that separated our house from Larry's. The bushes were nearly naked from the weeks of heat that had made their leaves give up and wither off, so it wasn't hard for me to squeeze among the branches. I moved further and further into the bushes, until I thought I could hear Marlene and Billy

Salzman breathing on the blanket they had spread beside the dried-up lilacs. They were breathing so loud, and I was crouched down so close, they didn't hear me aim my weapon and click it on. In the light, kissing with their eyes closed, they looked like one body, one face, and I couldn't tell whose head was whose, whose neck, whose back, whose sweaty hands. I couldn't tell where my sister stopped and Billy started—who was the hot one, who was the cold one, who was making who do what.

Then both of them blinked and turned in my direction.

I thought Marlene would kill me right then, just scratch her manicured fingernails across my heart so everything inside came pouring out.

But instead, she laughed and whispered in Billy's ear. She moved a few inches away from him and patted the blanket beside her.

"Come over here," she said. "Come sit with us."

I walked out of the azaleas and clicked off my flashlight. "I was looking for Larry. I thought he was back here."

"Oh," Marlene said. "I thought you were looking for me."

"I wasn't," I told her. "I'm not a baby. I don't need charity."

Billy was wearing a sleeveless white top that resembled an undershirt. The muscles on his arms looked like rocks that had been glued there. He lifted one arm and pointed out to our driveway.

"Isn't that Larry over there?" he said.

At the end of our driveway, Larry was standing on the fender of my father's convertible, babbling about how he had a perfect view of the flames downtown. But where we were, the sky was lit by stars alone.

The light from those stars lit the hairs under Billy's arm, not as many but as dark and as curly as the ones under my father's arms.

I tried to concentrate on Marlene's face. Her lips were shiny and wet, and I hoped Billy would catch her fever blister.

"Oh yeah," I said as I left them and crossed our yard. "That's Larry. Thanks a lot."

But I took my sweet time joining him. I went out to Keer Avenue and walked up and down the heat-cracked sidewalk, looking at the faces of the murmuring adults, like little white moons clustered on the stoops, and at the eaves of our houses as they turned to silhouettes against the bright night sky, and at my friends playing Statues on the front lawns and the curbs. Over near the corner, Larry was draped around a street lamp, with his head bent under his elbow.

"Hurry up, Debbie," he said when I got there. "I can't stay like this forever."

"Obviously," I told him, as someone grabbed my wrist. I shook free of the whirl and planted my feet on Keer Avenue. "No one can"

CONCESSIONS

Several years ago, I was returning a rented car at Newark Airport when I heard a radio report about the desecration of a Boston synagogue. Violent words had been spray-painted across the sanctuary, and the sacred Torah in its altar slashed and scattered in the street like a pack of torn-up lottery tickets. There was paint left over. Hurled by hoodlums on the run, the aerosol cans shattered every stained glass window. Prominent Bostonians immediately went on the air to express their shock and indignation, and listening to their voices *was* a comfort. But still, I felt a fear at once familiar and entirely strange, a vestigial and nearly physical foreboding.

A light snow was beginning as I boarded the shuttle from Newark back to Boston. That year, my parents were due up from Florida for a visit; their plane was scheduled to arrive at Logan Airport an hour after my own. I had felt it would be too much for my girls to spend the day at a graveyard in another state and then fly back to Boston to greet their grandparents, so I had gone alone to see my own grandfather—or, rather, to see his grave. He died many years ago, two days before Christmas, and I have gone to New Jersey, to the cemetery, every year since.

The funeral took place on a bitter cold afternoon, the air white as dry ice, the earth frigid as glass. That morning, everyone assembled at our house in Short Hills, where the mirrors had been covered with white sheets, according to the orthodox beliefs my grandfather had followed; later, we would sit on splintered crates instead of upholstered chairs. We were just about to leave for the mortuary when the people from the cemetery called to say they couldn't get any gravediggers until after the Christmas holiday. Ours was a Jewish cemetery, of course, but none of the workers was Jewish.

My mother's brother took the call. I never was told exactly how the matter was resolved. But I do know that Nat went down to the cemetery and spoke with someone, or with several people, and I imagine that large amounts of money crossed hands to ensure that the holiday season would be brighter for everyone involved. Or perhaps no money was needed for Nat to convince the gravediggers that it would be in their best interests, after all, to take up their shovels. Nat always had a way with words.

Michael waved as I entered the waiting area at Logan. The light snow was now nearly a blizzard. The observation deck had frosted up. The overhead monitors kept blinking "To Be Announced" or "Canceled." I made my way over and kissed him.

"How was it?" he asked.

I nodded. He patted my back as we hugged. "Are my parents going to make it?" I asked him.

"All the flights from Florida are canceled. Until some time tomorrow. Nobody's saying anything definite yet."

"Where are the girls?"

Michael held up their winter jackets and peered around the terminal. "Jemma? Larissa? Come on, girls. Let's go." He crushed the jackets to his chest and stared at me. "They were here just a minute ago."

I started hollering. "Jemma! Larissa!" I squeezed Michael's arm and tried to calm him. "Girls! Where are you?"

Once, when we were vacationing with my sister and her family on an unseasonably chilly June weekend, we had lost Jemma on a windy beach near Truro. I had run into the frigid ocean fully dressed, my lungs seared with fear. Knocked to my knees and turned around by the tide, I looked up to see Jemma building castles on top of the dunes.

Now I pushed my way through the crowded waiting area, talking to myself, breathing deeply during those last few seconds of calm, preparing for the worst.

On the far side of the terminal, a gaggle of children jiggled and twitched as they waited to talk to Santa Claus, enthroned on a red and green platform. Santa's assistant was handing out balloons and small bags of candies as the children left the bearded man's knee and went spinning, wide-eyed, back to their parents.

Behind the plastic ropes, my girls stood watching.

I waited a moment or so to steady myself before reaching out to tap their shoulders. Larissa stood transfixed, but Jemma blinked up at me and smiled.

"Hi, Mommy."

She turned back to the platform and kept watching Santa.

"Hi, Sweetheart," I said.

My hands had stopped trembling. I ran them along the nape of her neck and along the side of Lissa's cheek. Without looking up, Lissa swatted me lazily with her free arm and raised her tiny chin to whisper in her big sister's ear.

"It's not fair," she said.

Jemma nodded, biting her lip. I looked over their heads and saw Michael running toward us.

"Deborah! Did you find them?"

I pointed down, then over to Santa. Michael stood in a lacuna of space, staring at us. He let out his breath and stared at the jacket in his left hand, Jemma's plaid velour. He stared at the jacket in his right hand, Lissa's quilted corduroy with the padded bunny on the back.

"Jesus Christ," he said when he reached us.

Santa was bouncing twin boys, one on each knee. The airport Muzak meted out a creamy version of "Rudolph, the Red-Nosed Reindeer." Santa ho-ho-hoed and the crowd swayed in place. Lissa twisted her curls with her fingers and tugged at my sleeve. Jemma yanked her back to the border of plastic ropes.

"We can't," she said sharply. "How many times do I have to tell you?"

Michael left us in the terminal and went to get the Jeep, but when he came back, he said the engine had kicked over once and then given out. The waiting line for cabs stretched nearly to the next terminal, so I went inside and called my secretary, a man just a few years my junior named Joshua Stein. His parents used to be college professors but now they own their own cab; for years they have alternated the day and night shifts. Joshua said he could have whoever was driving come down and get us.

When I got back outside, I was relieved to see that the girls had recovered from Santa Claus. But now they were holding onto the No Parking pole at the loading zone as they swung round and round, their cheeks whipped by the cold wind, so I motioned them away from the curb and its death row of triple-parked cars and vans. Michael shuddered and peered into the traffic, the tip of his nose already reddening. In the army of cabs coming toward us, a particularly battered one stood out. "There's Mr. Stein," he said.

Joshua's father left the engine running as he walked toward us through the snow, spreading his hands in a wide, thick-fingered fan, as if he expected one of us to toss a beach ball his way. He motioned me into the cab's front seat while Michael got the girls into the back.

"Has the weather been like this all day?" I asked Mr. Stein as we headed toward the Callahan Tunnel. "Josh probably told you that I just flew back from Jersey. There was scarcely any snow down there."

Mr. Stein flicked a few coins into the toll bin and we squeezed into the dank incoming lane. "Josh told me you needed a ride from the airport." A crinkle of static came over the dispatcher to save him from further interrogation. "That's all he said. That's all I know."

He shrugged and lifted the microphone on the dashboard. "Millie?" he said.

Mr. Stein and his wife are aware of each other's whereabouts at nearly every moment, down to the street and the block. He nodded at the mike and the corners of his mouth eased into a smile.

"All right, doll," he said. "Whatever I do, I won't forget the Tropicana."

We had emerged from the tunnel. Mr. Stein motioned out at the congestion as we passed the historic stone buildings of Quincy Market, once the city's main mart and now heaven for holiday hordes. Everywhere I looked, Bostonians in heavy winter clothing scurried past, their arms laden with brightly-wrapped packages.

"Christmas traffic," said Mr. Stein. "This year I think I'm finally tired of it."

I turned in my seat to exchange glances with Michael, but he had pulled on his psychologist's face and was fiddling with the beeper at his waist. His features betrayed none of the surprise that Mr. Stein's words had made me feel. Relatively late in his life, Joshua has been attending Suffolk Law's night school while working as my legal seretary during the day. In the years I've known his parents, neither has ever revealed anything personal to me. What I know about the Steins has come from their son.

I shifted toward the view ahead. Because of the congestion, Mr. Stein had decided to take Storrow Drive, past an artless clump of buildings that once were luxury apartments but now were worn and faded. Instead of settling into second-rate, a giant billboard pointed out their one advantage: "If You Lived Here You'd Be Home By Now." Further up, the low twisting banks of the Charles ran along the solid press of brownstones that gives the Back Bay's outer limit the sense of natural cliffs.

In a few minutes our cab eased up to my building, a turquoise and caramel post-modern skyscraper with 365-degree views of the city. Since my parents' flight was canceled, I had decided to stop at the office for a few hours. Michael would bring the girls home. The day before, he had taken them skiing at Blue Hills, and they still were tired.

"Looks like your building is made of Play-Doh," Jemma piped up from the back seat as I got out. "Every time I come here, I start to think that you sell Play-Doh. I know it isn't true, but that's what I always think."

As Mr. Stein pulled away, I waved at the girls' grinning pink faces, pressed against the frosty rear window on either side of Michael. I tried not to think about all the holiday traffic and the slick icy roads that imperiled my family. In the cold orange sunset, I read the tattered old stickers on the taxi's back bumper: "Amandla," "Grandmothers for Choice," "Gorbachev for Governor." Some people make a career of camouflaging their politics, but I knew that the Steins had concealed themselves only during the Fifties, when they left Boston and lived for a month in each borough of New York City, and, for a while, with relatives in Schenectady who did not share their politics but, family being family, wanted the Steins to remain free to argue. Whenever Joshua's family moved, one of the boys was allowed to choose a new surname. Their parents would wake them in the middle of the night, offering chocolate milk and local telephone books. Whichever name the boys wanted was the name they went by until they moved again. By the time of his Bar-Mitzvah, Joshua had been everything from Ripley to Cooper to Gizeltheider to Currier. He learned his real last name after McCarthy was dead, when his family left Schenectady and came back to Boston.

Whenever I looked at the bumper stickers on the Steins' taxicab, I wanted to ask how, after all that, they retained enough hope even to hoist those small, obvious flags. They raised a family. They must have had fea

Later that night, my parents called to say that they were stranded in Philadelphia and would arrive the following evening. The airline had put up the passengers in luxury accommodations, and my parents were giddy as teenagers who had just won free tickets to a heavy metal concert. My mother had passed an unattended housekeeping cart, where she stocked up on miniature bottles of shampoo and fragrant bars of hotel soap. As we spoke, my father was debating which Pay-Per-View movie they would watch on the large-screen TV and charge to their corporate hosts.

I hung up the phone and went back to the stack of greeting cards on my desk. The week before, I had finished A to N. I had sent cards to all our friends in the first half of the alphabet and cards to all of Michael's relatives. Michael watched the news on television as I finished O to Z. The Commissioner of Police, speaking quietly, said the desecrators of the synagogue hadn't yet been apprehended. Then the Mayor and the Governor came on to promise that arrests were imminent. Downtown on the plaza outside of City Hall, a crowd of citizens gathered in the cold to register their shock and sadness at the crime. Several priests and reverends, and of course numerous well-known academics, shivered and spoke into microphones. Their faces looked truly pained.

For years, Michael had been after me to list our home number in the telephone book or to put our return address on mail I send out. But these were things I simply couldn't do. No one in my family did. When I was small, when my father worked for my Uncle Nat, I asked about it once. Whatever answer I was given must have made a kind of sense—or at least, a strong impression. I couldn't recall the answer now, and so I always felt frustrated when Michael asked me to explain.

When the news ended, he raised the issue again. "I'm worried about the effect on the girls," he said. "How can their friends call them if they can't look up the phone number?"

On television, Natalie Jacobson and Chet Curtis were debating the weather: probably a record-breaking storm within the next twenty-four hours, she said; maybe not, he said. Natalie and Chet are married, and so their gentle disagreements always seemed natural. But Chet was living in a dream world that night. Outside, the snow hurtled.

"What's Kim's last name?" I asked Michael. I turn amnesiac on people's surnames, but never their faces or connection to us.

"Kim and Charles, down the street."

"Hers is Johnson and his is Cooke. But you're changing the subject."

"I can't explain, okay? We've been through this. It's just an old habit. Like I don't cook pork or shellfish. It's just—the way I was raised, okay? Don't make it into a federal case."

"You don't cook pork, but you eat it at Chinese restaurants. And at the Cape, you eat lobster. You love lobster."

"Now you've got me. You've nailed me. Happy? Yes, I love lobster. I confess. I'm a person with contradictions—but I'm sure you've run into that phenomenon before. That's what you *do*, Michael. That's your profession. Anyway, the girls are too young to make their own social arrangements. And all the parents know our phone number."

"Could you at least try to talk about this reasonably? Could you try not to take it so personally?"

I left the stack of greeting cards and headed for the stairs. "Of course I'm trying. I'm always trying," I told him.

In the kitchen, I made some hot chocolate. While the water was boiling, I got out the ammonia and cleaned the Corian, just as my mother used to clean the mirrored door in our living room on Keer Avenue when she couldn't sleep. But I always keep the lights off in case the girls wake up—I don't want them thinking that the only way a grown woman can calm herself is by cleaning.

When the kitchen was clean, I brought the mugs upstairs and found Michael in their room, smoothing Jemma's blanket and patting its edges under the mattress. Across the room, Lissa's feet dangled in mid-air, her pale forehead pressed against the footboard. I went over and lifted her head back onto the pillows. Michael reached for me, but I went to the window and looked down at our street. Outside, a few of our neighbors were sprinkling salt from large sacks onto the frozen front walks and driveways. From where I stood,

I could see a slice of the center of Lexington and the spire of the clap-board church that Paul Revere passed as he rode from Concord to Boston. The snow was falling and scarcely any traffic moved on Massachusetts Avenue, the artery that runs through Lexington, Arlington, Cambridge, and into Boston.

Michael came over and put his arm around me. I leaned my head on his shoulder.

"I'm worried about my parents' flight," I told him. "I'm worried that the plane will crash in this mess."

"Honey. The plane's not even in the air. Your parents are in a luxury hotel, happily charging room service and cable TV. And by tomorrow the police will catch whoever desecrated that synagogue."

"No one works this close to Christmas. Not even cops. Especially not cops."

"Then they'll find them the day after Christmas."

"You know what really gets me?" I asked him. "It's always the Reform temples that get hit. You'd think it would be the Orthodox *shul*—but, no. The Reform temples get hit more often."

"Meaning?"

"Don't analyze me. You know I hate that. It's just an observation."

A group of carolers came up the street, holding candles at the darkness. Faintly I heard the start of "Silent Night," my favorite of the season. Michael hummed a bar or two and pulled me closer.

"Maybe it's time to ask your father what he did for a living," he said.

"He owned a tavern in Newark. Which you know."

"I meant, how he got started. What your Uncle Nat did—how he actually earned a living. How your father helped him."

"My Uncle Nat was in concessions. As you also know."

"Ask your father what 'concessions' really meant."

At Jemma's bed, I smoothed down the final wrinkle in her blanket. I adjusted the shade on the night-light, which Lissa had skewed with her foot. Then I walked back to Michael and whispered.

"You think that's the answer. You think you can ask people rational questions and in enough time, with enough of your patience, they'll answer, as if they're bound by solemn oath to tell the truth and nothing but, and then you'll understand everything."

"What happens when the girls ask us?"

In the darkness, I couldn't see his face. In silhouette, he might have been any stranger.

"Ask us what? Ask why people write dirty words on synagogue walls? What's the answer, will you please tell me? Tell me, what answer can you give your daughters?"

My parents' plane landed the following night. Because the roads still were dangerous, they insisted on taking a cab out from Logan instead of letting us pick them up. I asked Joshua to send one of his parents, and the cab arrived at our house just as the girls were finishing their baths and getting ready for bed.

My father wore his feathered fedora and gray topcoat. He stood in the doorway and somehow survived Jemma's running jump into his arms, while my mother knelt and enfolded Lissa into the satin lining of her fur coat. Lissa waited until Michael had gone into the kitchen to heat water for tea. She glanced at me slyly and turned back to her grandparents.

"Did you bring us anything?"

Jemma, older by twenty-eight months, made a slight show of decorum, twisting the flounced hem of her nightie as she stared eagerly up.

"Girls," I told them. "You know that's rude."

My parents had brought educational coloring books, huge sets of pastels in wooden boxes, and ten silver dollars apiece—most likely from Nassau, where they flew from Florida for at least one weekend a month. The girls laid the silver dollars on the living room carpet, making piles of two, then of five, then of ten. They opened the wooden boxes and stacked the pastels alongside, counting the colorful sticks with whoops and cheers, astonished more by multitude than value. "Twenty altogether," they kept saying, slapping their palms on their powdery foreheads. It was hard to tell if they were talking about the pastels or the dollars. "Twenty altogether!"

"I wish those things still were solid silver." My father picked up a coin and pointed to the copper inset. "That way it would be an investment. This way it's just twenty bucks."

He tossed the dollar back onto the carpet.

"Leave it to Uncle Sam to fix something that ain't broke," he said.

In the morning, the girls raced down the hallway, demanding a demonstration of dice tricks, while I followed with their toothbrushes. My mother had gone downstairs to start breakfast and Michael was in the shower. I sat in the rocker, watching my father motion Jemma toward his opened suitcase. She pulled out a small leather case and waved it as she stepped across the mattress.

"One trick," my father said. Lissa, pressed against his chest, twisted her face in mock torture. "One trick only," he told her. "After that, you two go off with your mother and brush your teeth. Promise?"

He opened the leather case and produced several pairs of dice, some translucent red, some translucent green—these reminded me of Chuckles jellies, dotted with white circles instead of sugar granules—and a few standard ivory pairs. With what appeared to be some joint pain, he got out of bed and knelt on the carpet. He tossed the dice against the wall; the girls roared and swooned as he made whichever number they called out come up, again and again, and again.

It was the morning of Christmas Eve. Michael had had the Jeep repaired and I planned to go into the office for a few hours while he took the girls to show off to my parents what they had learned on the ski slopes at Blue Hills. So far, no legs or necks had been broken. But I wasn't at all reassured as we sat down to breakfast and Jemma described the sensation of gliding across the kiddy slope.

"It's so-o-o-o dangerous," she said. "It's the most dangerous thing I've ever done."

Lissa leaned her chin on her palm and stared up at my father. "Did you ever go skiing?"

"No, he never did." My mother held up a spoonful of Cream of Wheat as Lissa inched against her. Lissa opened her mouth and kept talking while my mother ladled in the cereal.

"Did you ever do anything dangerous?"

"Depends upon your point of view," my father said.

My mother gave him a look.

"But never on purpose," he added. She leaned over and wiped cereal from Lissa's chin. Jemma said, "What do you mean?"

"Adult things," my father said. "But I never went skiing, and I never would. I'm too big a coward to try getting anywhere with wooden sticks on my feet."

"They make you go faster." Jemma laughed. "They're not scary at all. They make you fly! We'll teach you how. Lissa and I will show you."

"No thanks. Watching the both of you, such big brave girls, will be enough of a thrill for one day."

"Maybe some other time," my mother told them.

The few people who remain in my office toward the end of December either are new to the firm, or they don't celebrate Christmas. I walked past a squat comb of quarter-walled cubicles where a handful of junior associates bent over their desks, each one as reticent to speak as the homeless who duck into public libraries for warmth at this time of year, and entered my corner office. I spent a few hours reading memos and answering phone messages from acquaintances who wanted to reciprocate the first batch of greeting cards I had sent but were unable to write us at home or to call there.

Every few minutes, Joshua came to my door to ask if I needed anything, slightly embarrassed to find he wasn't interrupting me. Joshua has notions of how things should be when a person like me reaches a position like this, and the fact that my pace never is killing, never as difficult as his parents', mystifies and somewhat unnerves him.

Late in the day, on his way out, he pointed to the new building going up across the street. "Look at that," he said in admiration. "Isn't that terrific?"

I swiveled in my chair and watched two gleaming Caterpillars with metal belts as wide as rivers move along the snowy earth. The new building was made of glass, steel, and something that seemed to me adobe, although reason says it must have been a different substance. From the fourth to the sixth story, a huge space had been excised from front to back and planted with a trio of exotic full-grown trees that seemed to float in mid-air, as though Magritte or Dali dreamed them. Whatever type of trees they were, those three were not local to Massachusetts.

But no matter. The trees had taken root. The building's prize-winning architect had won a national competition and promised Boston's city fathers a showpiece as urbane and innovative as one in Houston or Miami: an edifice that would be, somehow, both postmodern and indigenous.

"It's interesting," I told Joshua, although to me the building looked incongruous, a futuristic foray in a city strongly linked to past. I have noticed that New England seems to exert a special pull on people like me, who come here for college from the Mid-Atlantic states and decide to stay—as though the area indelibly reaffirms, year after year and in more vibrant color, the memories that New Jersey and New York obscure in increasing gray. Even the name "New England" seems to grant the states within it a true and lasting presence, while "Mid-Atlantic" is a relative term, a name that is not here, not there.

But the construction site evidently filled Joshua with a feeling far different than mine, and truer in its essence than simple-minded civic pride. Born here, Joshua had stayed in place, except for the years of the McCarthy period. Over time, he had watched Boston change into something different but not by definition worse. There probably was no single moment when he noticed how altered was the area from what he recalled of it; the city simply had grown up as a child does, moment by moment, day by day, in nuances nearly imperceptible to those who are nearby.

For me, it was as difficult to accept Boston's bustling new identity as it would be for a parent to forgive a child who runs away and returns, bizarrely, as a perfectly well-adjusted adult.

When I got home from the office, I found a gift-wrapped package on our doorstep, with a tag that said "To the Tarlow-Carrs." I tossed my coat on the banister and brought the package into the kitchen, calling for Michael, for the girls, for my parents. On the tag, our neighbor Kim Johnson had written: "To the four of you from the four of us. Sorry about what's missing from this. But it's the thought that counts, even if Courtney can't!"

Courtney was the Johnsons' youngest. She had made us a brown clay menorah with seven instead of eight holders for candles.

Hanukah had been over for weeks, but I set the menorah on the living room mantle and went upstairs to see where everyone was. I checked our bedroom, the girls' room, the guest room. I looked in the bathrooms. And I tried not to look in the closets, but I did look in a few. The faint outline of the moon was growing visible when I went to the window seat in the hallway and stared down at the pre-Revolutionary colonials on our winding street. The glass was frosting over and the lights had begun to flick on in several neighbors' houses. Fresh trees invigorated most of the living rooms, alongside slate fireplaces. The Johnsons' windows were bunted with artificial snow, but only a cluster of poinsettias in silvery pots graced their mantle. When Michael and I

first were married and living in Watertown, each Christmas the fa-
cades of the tightly-packed houses were layered in multi-colored lights
until long after New Year's—their doorways, windows, even ridge poles
strung with the gaudy bright of what in its essence is a religion born of
awe at quiet modesty, at simple virtues. In Lexington, the houses are
much larger than in Watertown. The front lawns sloped languorously
and on none of them did I see a neon Santa, nor a reindeer-drawn
sleigh. No mangers. No Magi. It seemed obvious to me that humility
arrived with greater surety to those who had the most to worry over
and protect.

I looked again at the sky, thick with the undertow of steely gray that
comes before the second, harsher snowfall of the season. Our house
sits atop a fairly high hill, and in the distance, Boston's skyline seemed
a sanctum both for those whose credo was "Goodwill Toward Men"
and the roving bigots who still had not been apprehended. The moon
that night was nearly full. Its shadings had acquired more depth, more
height and fall, than only moments earlier. On Monday, Michael had
driven me over to Blue Hills to reassure me about the kiddy slope.
Now, staring out at lunar ruts and valleys, I saw the girls hurtling down,
not stopping, until they flew into the stars and crashed onto their ski
poles, bloodily impaled upon our aspirations for them.

But the two orbs of white coming toward me were the headlights of
his car, proceeding carefully along our thickly-salted road. He pulled
up to our driveway, turned off the ignition, and peered up at me as my
mother opened the back door for the girls. My father got out of the
front passenger seat and reached to remove their tiny four skis from
the overhead rack. The girls tumulted out from the back.

I pressed my face against the window's cool glass. Then I went
downstairs to the kitchen.

"What were you doing up there?"
Michael was hanging his coat in the mud room as Jemma and
Lissa stomped snow from their boots and unzipped their parkas.

"You looked like a ghost," he told me. "You nearly scared me to
death."
Jemma yanked off Lissa's boots and when she had done, Lissa
yanked off her sister's, stuck her hands inside and clapped the boots

together. Their faces were bright from the cold.

I glanced over their snowy heads at Michael. "Where the hell were you so long? You were supposed to be back hours ago."

"I told you I was taking the girls to the dentist after Blue Hills. No big deal. Remember? They needed check-ups and Bert had a last-minute cancellation."

"'*No big deal?*' Three hours later and it's no big deal? They could have been killed!"

Jemma motioned Lissa to put the boots in the rack and the two girls slid away.

"Killed how?" my father was saying, behind me. "With a dentist's drill?"

"Not now, Vic," my mother told him.

"I was standing right there. That guy couldn't have tried anything."

"I've been worried sick," I told Michael.

"You worry too much, Sweetheart. Always did," my father said.

"Why didn't you call?" I asked Michael.

Behind me Jemma said, "I didn't have any cavities. Neither did Larissa. Aren't you proud of us?"

"It's the fluoride in the water," said my father. "Those Commies had the right idea about that all along."

One of the girls' parkas had fallen to the mud room floor. Michael hung it back on its hook and tried not to laugh.

"For Christ's sake," I said to the three of them. "What is wrong with all of you?"

The girls padded into the living room, their double layers of socks trailing watery snow. Michael turned his head and studied me.

"You are shouting," he said. "You are shouting at me and at your parents, and you are frightening both of our daughters."

"Good-looking trees," my father said a few minutes later, after I announced that I was going out to get some air. When he offered to come, I banged the screen door behind me. I walked slowly to let him catch up and now, side by side, we were approaching Lexington Center, its fine markets and shops closed early for the holiday.

He pointed to the Common's edge. "I don't think I've ever seen trees like those."

Concessions

The frosty overhanging branches were postcard-perfect. Against the falling snow, they seemed drawn in pen-and-ink by an artist with a large and steady hand.

"They're sycamores," I told him. "Some are maples. Of course you've seen them. They're common all along the Eastern seaboard."

It was not a particularly cold night by New England standards, but my father's teeth chattered as he took a monogrammed handkerchief from the pocket of his topcoat and wiped the corners of his eyes.

"People walk by things every day and don't have a clue what they're seeing," he told me. "They don't want to know."

We cut across the empty Common, besieged during daylight by awe-struck tourists and bundled schoolchildren lined up in homage. On both sides of the walkway, statues of Revolutionary heroes peered stoically down from their granite pedestals. In another few minutes, we neared the post office. A white-haired couple was leaving as we walked in, their facial skin fretted with delicate creases, like tissue paper saved and reused from season to season. But their spines were straight as they headed back into the night—the sort of couple common in this area, retired professors from Harvard or MIT, people who summer up in Bar Harbor or down in calm Nantucket. They walked arm in arm into the snow with great vigor, as if talking and thinking for all those years had done something wonderful and irreversible for their muscle tone.

The main section was closed but the door to the post office lobby was open, the few strands of modest holiday lights at the windows casting a dignified yellow-white glow. Along the far wall, the rental boxes came in three sizes, their identification numbers jumbled, as if arranged according to some secret order. My father bit at the tips of his gloves and pulled them off, breathing into his palms and rubbing them together.

I stood at the zip-code books along the far windows and gave him some time to warm up.

"I wonder how they arrange those boxes," I said. "There doesn't seem to be a pattern."

It took him only moments to figure it out. "Sure there's a pattern! Look." He waved his arms at the metal boxes as he explained the pattern, as if the boxes ached, and over time his hands had acquired the power to heal.

He was right, of course. I saw it as soon as he said it. "Short Hills was full of sycamores," I told him.

"'Short Hills,'" he repeated, as if the town he had struggled all his life to reach was a theme park in a state he couldn't quite recall ever having visited. Both of us gazed up at the ceiling. Somehow, I noticed, a huge wad of chewing gum had gotten stuck near the overhead fixture.

"'Short Hills.' That's right. Maybe I did run into a few fancy trees in that place, but figured them fronts for something else."

Then he looked back toward the rows of numbered boxes. Turned at an angle, he added, "Listen to me, Deborah. This is nothing you don't know. I was a spit-poor kid from the worst part of Newark—even then, it was a jungle. Not much older than your Lissa when my father died. My mother died when I was Jemma's age, *Aleha ha Shalom.* May she rest in peace. I'm not making excuses, I'm just reporting the facts. By the time we moved to Short Hills, I was middle-aged. All I knew was how to earn a living, how to survive. Not a skill that you yourself ever needed to develop, thank the Lord. And it led to many problems with your mother. As you know. But all I knew to do was work. That's all. I didn't have any hobbies. When was I supposed to get them? Now I don't know how to be retired. Always figured I'd be dead before I got to be retired. It's not easy to appreciate new things, Sweetheart. Even if they're the right things. That's the reason people have children."

I thought of Jemma and Larissa, his youngest grandchildren, and the hot bath that Michael at that very moment probably was foisting on them to coax the cold of skiing from their bones. At first, they would protest loudly. This act was a tradition. Then, after being in the water for a while, they would refuse to get out.

"Having two children, you ought to understand what I'm saying," my father told me.

Case closed. He shrugged and lifted a Dunhill cigar from his pocket. At least, his face shrugged. Although he was a large man, he had always used his body economically, almost delicately—he never was the sort to involve his shoulders in something that could be handled more privately. Our walk had been short, but it had strained him, and as he came toward me, he gasped for breath.

"How did you get started?" I asked him. "What did 'concessions' really mean?"

He unwrapped the cigar, slipped off the gold paper ring, and patted it into his pocket. "For my girls." He winked. "I used to do the same thing for you and your sister. Remember?" He plucked the Dunhill from his mouth and rotated it between his two fingers, the ash grown thick and long as his brown-stained thumbnail. "Not a word to your mother," he said. Then he reached back into his pocket, came up with a small vial of nitroglycerine tablets, and slid a tablet under his tongue.

In that yellow-white light, the public light of funeral parlors and interrogation rooms, his pale skin and rheumy eyes brought back my grandfather at his cobbler's bench, mourning the dearth of fine horses on Newark's dense streets, and later, lying in the unadorned pine coffin that smelled like the boardwalk at Asbury Park. Mahogany was smoother, but the unfinished pine had been required by the tenets of my grandfather's orthodoxy. The pine box, the silky fringed shroud over my grandfather's body and the white headdress folded into a fan around his face: all of it had happened to him overnight, according to an ancient protocol I scarcely understood. I had stood saying good-bye with my hand on the edge, fearing the danger of splinters on such old, tired flesh. I kept hoping he would realize that the pine meant we loved him no less than if it were a sacrilegious steel coffin lined in tufted satin.

My father sidled his fingers forward on his Dunhill, as if to reason with it—just a simple word or two—and that trunk of ash went silently to the post office floor.

"So," he said. "What was it that you asked me?"

The nitroglycerine had done its job. His breathing had turned calm now. I waved away the Dunhill's smoke.

"You shouldn't smoke those things," I said. "They're sure to kill you."

"That's excellent advice. But sooner or later, something's got to. Am I right, *Consigliere?*"

The snow still was falling, but bits of dark sky were returning to vision as we stepped into the cold night air. On Lexington Common, the statues of heroes were coated in white, their stories shrouded in myth for over two centuries. Long ago, during Christmas, a large cross might have topped the venerable evergreen towering on the Common. But now my daughters were free to enjoy summer picnics beneath the statues' shadows, their dark hair freshly braided and their pinkened torsos and limbs refreshed in cool cotton play suits. Lexington is a conservative town in terms of natural temperament, lately liberal in its politics—once revolutionary, now enshrined. An historic compromise between the past and the future: making safe for posterity what had been truly dangerous. This monumental change had been accomplished without debate or fanfare, with the dynamic ease of natural process, the way a flame beneath the surface eventually will force that surface to the air, the way the earth appears to be stable when actually it is spinning, always, on its axis further into time.

A block from the house, a red Studebaker in perfect condition came slowly up the street, making fresh tracks in the snow. The elderly couple we had seen at the post office looked familiar to me now, the man with his arms straight out at the wheel and the woman bent beside him in the passenger seat, aiming a flashlight at an opened road map. The map made me think that the couple was going to celebrate Christmas with distant relatives, and it felt good to imagine that, at their ages, they still had enough family that the route wasn't familiar.

Toot-toot went the horn as the Studebaker drew even with us.

"Merry Christmas!" they cried.

On the glazed sidewalk ahead, my father was skidding as he gathered loose snow. He packed a ball the size of a grapefruit, tossed it my way and held his hands in front of his face.

"Merry Christmas," I called, and bent to the ground, gathering loose snow in my turn.

But instead of throwing my snowball, I climbed to the top of our driveway. That morning, Michael had borrowed a snow blower and aimed it uphill, then used our Jeep to carve a cross-hatch of treading that tamped down the loose drifts. Every year, we debated buying a blower, or even a small plow like the Kendalls', next door. We'll never do either, of course—we're doing fine. In winter, the snow dissolves the property lines and links us together, the descendants of long-standing privilege with newcomers like us, equally, here.

I stepped to where the edge of the driveway slopes into a ravine that snakes below the yards on our side of the street. A few hardy sycamores clutched to the cleft, nearly hidden by the blur of snow that kept falling between their bare branches, filling cold space. Among the rocks protruding from the frozen stream, a wooden sled lay nearly buried, its runners two slices of shining ice. Everything smelled fresh and wet, but somewhere there was smoke: the Kendalls' chimney signaling a message, and then I saw another, further down the block. Michael had started a fire, and smoke was curling from our chimney, too.

I moved as near to the edge as I dared. I told myself that I could see down to the ivied brick bastion of Harvard, across the Charles River to the puritanical spire of Olde North Church, clear to the gilt dome of the State House. From where I stood, the suburbs and city seemed inextricably linked, more powerful together than apart, the head and the heart of the same place in time. The scene was Baroque, with no single center, no piece that excised would leave it as vital. Out here, we are miles from Boston, but it was as if I could touch all that organized clutter, all that human endeavor stretching toward the blue-black Harbor, and all of its traditional tensions surrendered for now to the white flag of winter. On such a fine night, it was easy to see why Bostonians insist on calling this city "The Hub," as if the rest of New England, or even the universe, willingly and long ago acquiesced to its own view.

In truth, a wind had come up and I couldn't see or hear very much of anything. Everything was whiteness, silent whiteness, until, somewhere in the distance, church bells rang and echoed. Soon, we would celebrate the secular New Year. Yet I thought I heard the ancient *shofar* of Jerusalem: low, long, incandescent, a joyous sob of grief and hope. I thought I heard the falling snow around me.

Sometimes, I think that I was born agnostic. But the notion of creation, of starting something that cannot be stopped by a stroke of luck, good or bad: this, I believe in.

In fact, I do not believe at all in luck. Only, with certainty, in the forces that we ourselves, with our own hands, cup to our lips and set into motion.

I lifted my arm to the moon, to the widening sky and the stars that glowed there. My snowball rose and hovered, a small planet savoring the cold air, until gravity forced it to settle. That year, on Christmas Eve in Massachusetts, I felt relieved and amazed that the circumstances of life had granted the people I loved what seemed, at that moment, such safe and privileged shelter.

THE ORPHAN

"*Cremated?* What the hell was Beaver thinking?"

My father lies on stiff white sheets, his legs straight out, the bed's top half cranked sharply at an angle. He is gripping the obituary pages of *The Suburban Jewish News*, which publishes from Livingston, New Jersey, but started out, like all of us, years ago in Newark.

"Jews don't get cre*mat*ed," he reminds me, stressing the middle syllable to emphasize his contempt for the way his oldest brother ended. "Not voluntarily, they don't. Plus: both of my parents were orthodox. The orthodox have to be buried. In a plain pine box. Everybody knows that."

"I didn't even know that your parents were religious," I tell him.

"In Israel they forget the box, and just stick with the shroud. Oh, sure," he says. "You kidding? That whole generation."

My paternal grandfather died when my father was a boy, and so I never met him, or my paternal grandmother, either. She died a few years later, orphaning my father when he was only ten. I did meet both of his older brothers. For a while, when I was a child, we lived in the same building as his middle brother, Harry, and his family. Then my father began to make a success of himself, and we moved to a better part of Newark. Eventually, we moved out to Short Hills. We saw his side of the family less and less.

Now, several decades later, his oldest brother, Beaver, has pulled his final disappearing act.

"Gone up in smoke without a trace," my father says.

His Head stays angling downward, his eyes still focused on those paragraphs printed and unchanging fact. I move over to his side, in the space between the bed and the night stand. I try to imagine learning of my sister's death by opening a newspaper from a place we used to live.

"I'm sorry, Pop," I tell him.

Without looking up, he pats the hem of the sun dress I changed into at the airport. "I just hope that you and Marlene never pull a stunt like cremation on me," he warns. "Don't even think about it. If the real Messiah finally shows up, He'll bring you back to life. That's the deal." Then he takes a manicure scissors from the night stand and carefully cuts out Beaver's obituary. He eases his legs to the floor, slips his feet into a pair of paper slippers, and shuffles to the hospital robe hanging on a hook behind the door. "P.S.," he adds as he shimmies into the robe. "And He'll need the bones to do it. Even a Messiah can't do much with ashes." With the side of one palm, he slides a small dune of loose change on the dresser into his other palm. He tilts his filled palm; the weight sags the frayed robe by several inches as the coins slant to the pocket. He tucks Beaver's obituary in the other pocket, spits at both palms, and rubs them over his temples. His wispy hair won't settle. Even in the Sixties, when men his age wore leisure suits and let their hair grow free, he stayed loyal to his faintly iridescent suits and still slicked down his hair.

"I need my Vitalis," he says.

His voice is plaintive and unfathoming, a child's. He must hear it, too, because after a moment, he turns back to me, recovers himself and becomes again my father.

"We'll go upstairs and get you something to eat," he says. "It's dog food, but at least it'll fill your stomach." Finally, as if the two of them will be there waiting in the cafeteria, he adds, "You remember your uncles, don't you, Sweetheart?"

His expression is so yearning that I want to lie and reassure him that I do, that I still can see every feature on their faces, every bone and muscle. But it's really smoke and ashes I recall. Next month, my father will turn seventy. When he last saw his brothers, he was younger than I am now; and I was just a girl. After so much time, Beaver is a blur to me.

What I remember of the middle brother, Harry, is more clearly focused: the world's longest legs bending to a squat; two powerful arms that sailed me toward a ceiling somewhere over dying Newark; the lips that brushed my cheek as I rose above the others. This childish view of heaven—being, for a blissful moment, taller than my sister—is what survives in memory of a man I never really knew. He and Beaver and my father were smoking Macanudos, creating one large cumulus of bluish smoke that shrouded their three faces, the white ash falling fine as ocean spray from the tips of their cigars. Mid-air, I spied a squadron of Manischewitz bottles on a rented table, its scarred surface camouflaged by a blue and white paper cloth meant to look like Israel's flag. This must have been a holiday, a rare Passover. We spent all the other holidays, and most *seders*, with my mother's side.

On Passover, Jews are enjoined to *remember when we were slaves in Egypt*, to remember all of history—but now, I can only see my uncles masked by that cigar smoke. Still, I always loved the thought of them. I loved to think my orphaned father hadn't been entirely alone.

"Can I see the obituary?" I ask.

My father takes it from his pocket and unfolds it. "Do you think the picture's any good?" He is leaning over my shoulder as I read. "Seems to me he's put on weight. Don't you think he looks more like Harry here than me? And see how he smiles that half-smile, won't fully open his mouth? That's because Beaver always hated his teeth."

My father's teeth are a source of pride to him. Only one is false. He lost that tooth after his mother died, when he spent his nights squatting in a steel cage above the gleaming pins at Newark's Golden Bowling. One night, the kid in the next cage took too long to lean out and reset; the exploding pins broke both his legs. My father turned to look, and lost his tooth. Then he went back to work in his cage. Eventually, he saved enough for dentistry, and a tavern in the Central Ward. "Top of the line," he still says about that tooth. And it's true that only an expert could tell which one it is.

"Beaver thought his lousy teeth ruined his whole kisser. 'Get them fixed,' I used to say to him.'You're a high roller, a *guntsa-knocker.*' Once, I dragged him to my guy, a combo ortho-periodontist, a real pro. But when Beaver found out what the guy charged, that was the end of that. So that's what you get when you're tight with the dollar. At the end, you can't open your mouth. Come on, let's go upstairs. You must be starving."

It's far too warm in here; cardiac patients cannot tolerate air-conditioning. I'm sweating in my sleeveless dress, but my father is trembling in his hospital robe. I can almost hear his own teeth chattering.

"I think you should check with the nurses first," I tell him.

"This is a hospital, not a prison. And you're still the daughter, not the parent. Let's go. My treat."

"Go tell someone, or else I will."

"I know that tone. The big-shot lawyer. Picking on your poor old father."

"You're seventy. Not even. Come on, Pop. Please."

He makes a show of sighing, then wanders off to get permission for our expedition. I walk over to the wall of window, where the light is brighter. Outside, on the corner, a *minyan* of old men in short-sleeved shirts and Bermuda shorts is gathering beneath the bus stop's corrugated roof, On days like this, so far from home, the burning sun could kill them.

I turn and squint at the obituary. Yes, Harry is alive. And he still lives in Jersey, in fact still is "of Union," an unpretentious town just down Morris Avenue from Short Hills, the fancy one my family moved to after Newark burned in 1967. If I call the newspaper and explain, perhaps they'll help me find a way to him. The brothers haven't talked in years, but seeing Harry might rejuvenate my father.

"No dice," he says a second later. "We can't go upstairs."

He's back in the doorway, clutching at his robe. He jabs a nicotine-stained thumb, a relic of the time when he could freely smoke his Macanudos, towards the nurse who stands beside him.

"I guess you'll have to starve to death," he tells me. "According to Eva Braun here, I'm not busting out. Not even two flights up."

But I can tell he likes her, and she knows it, from the way she rolls her eyes and wags a finger back at him.

"This is coronary care," the nurse reminds him. "Not a resort, Mr. Tarlow. Not a casino. We don't go in for gambling. We don't like the odds." She turns to me and smiles brightly. "You must be his younger daughter. He talks a lot about you and your sister. If you'd like, we can go and talk, and I can fill you in on the facts."

Now I'm forced to look down at the huge chart she is holding.

"He's still very much at risk," she adds, tapping a manicured finger at its sturdy plastic cover. "He needs to rest. You and I can talk, and you can come back later for another visit."

The Orphan

She seems a perfectly fine person, a professional who is trying. But I don't want to hear the facts. They never add up to what's supposed to happen, anyway. Then I know I must go, for my father's sake.

"Besides, you need to move your bowels," she tells him.

What is there to say, what words of comfort can be offered to a man who must be thus instructed by a woman who is less than half his age? My father doesn't utter anything, not a syllable of rebellion. So I take him in my arms and press my lips against the smooth skin of his cheek, just below his temple. The ambulance came straight here when he collapsed, so he has no Old Spice with him. But all those years of application have eased into his flesh, like a relic oiled through the centuries. I hold him close and whisper that, tonight, I'll find a way to get the girls in. They're with Michael, at my mother's condominium complex, swimming in the pool beside the ocean.

"How will I find him?" my father mumbles in my ear. "How will I find his grave if there's only ashes?"

But before I can respond, or even fully realize he means Beaver, my father has stepped away. He is belting out instructions to me for the nurse's benefit.

"When you come back, bring a decent robe and slippers, and some Vitalis," he says. "The bottle's on the bathroom sink. And bring my toothpaste, and my floss. Don't forget the toothpaste. The stuff they give you in this joint tastes like poison. I wouldn't give it to my worst enemy, let alone put it in my mouth. When they nabbed me, those *shmendricks* must have dropped my keys. But talk to Marvin Glickman, he's the owner of the Bay Brook. He's a *goniff*, a real thief, but he'll let you in." I'll buy everything he needs at the hotel; I won't go near that bungalow court. Two months ago, after his first heart attack, Marlene was the one who flew down here. She went to the bungalow court to get a few of my father's things, and warned me to avoid it.

The nurse, whose name is Susan, leads me to a half-walled cubicle just a few yards from my father's room and I take a seat across from her at a small, polished metal table. This hospital is part of a for-profit chain, and I didn't want him here. But the center where he kills the time by playing poker with some guys from Jersey is wired to this place—probably every place in Dade or Broward County is wired to some hospital or other—and he arrived in less than seven minutes. That's what the profit motive does, said my father proudly when I called from Boston.

All the patient rooms on this floor, Cardiac Care, are arranged in a semi-circle. Susan and I are sitting near the epicenter, one slice of a pie-shaped bank of gleaming stainless desks, a kind of high-tech cockpit. Radiating outward is a crew of sharp-eyed technicians, their suntanned poker faces all turned up. Above, suspended by steel rods, a universe of devices is blinking every color in the spectrum, monitoring those patients still worth an investment.

Medical people often treat lawyers with a palpable chilliness, but I must admit that Susan is thorough and compassionate. With what clearly is genuine feeling, she gives me my father's prognosis, which is terrible. His heart's too damaged now for intervention. But if I wait just a while—would I like some herbal tea or flavored decaf coffee?—she'll page someone from my father's team of cardiologists to tell me more.

"Maybe later, when my husband comes," I somehow manage to express to her as we shake hands good-bye.

Outside, in the hospital's vast parking lot, the humidity is murderous. I have to wade across a boiling sea of cars that will never know a spot of rust before I find the one we rented. Thank God it's air-conditioned. Thank God it's a Buick, progeny of General Motors. We had to rent GM, because I knew my father would be checking. He never has forgiven Henry Ford for his raging anti-Semitism.

Sure enough, my father is standing at his wall of window when I squint up and finally spot him. I wave and point towards the Buick; he gives me the thumbs-up sign. I try to motion that he ought to step away now, lie down on the bed and rest, but he won't budge. He's still standing at the window when I pull out in the Buick, flick on the air conditioning and drive slowly past the old men huddled at the bus stop—who, I realize as I near them, look very much like the photograph of Beaver, and not unlike my father. All these men could be related.

I take the obituary from my pocket and place it on the seat beside me. If *The Suburban Jewish News* can't give me Harry's whereabouts, maybe I can get his number from northern Jersey information.

By the time I have driven from the hospital back to the hotel,

The Orphan

Michael and the girls have returned from my mother's. Everyone has showered and changed into dry clothes. Shyly, the girls offer me bits of shells and driftwood that they found along the beach beside the pool; they don't know what words to give me. Michael has ordered a few appetizers from room service, but when I tell him I can't eat a thing, the girls insist that they're not hungry, either— another offering that pains me. So I say that I am starving for some real food, not just snacks, and we go down to the patio restaurant on the ocean, where the liveliness of the suntanned diners lets the girls begin to chatter and eat guiltlessly.

Their dessert has just arrived when my mother shows up. I push away a plate of food I haven't touched and spot her speaking to the maitre'd, who points in our direction. Michael and the girls must also know the reason that she's here, or else they read it in my eyes. Suddenly, they're absolutely silent, the girls' laden spoons of ice cream frozen in mid-air. My mother nods her thanks and slowly starts to make her way to us; I slide back my chair and stand.

Ever since my father's first heart attack, I have been unable to talk to my mother. Before then, I didn't take sides. That their retirement was hell for both my parents, I found wholly credible. My father had worked so much when my sister and I were growing up that my mother must have completed her grieving and deluded herself into thinking she already was, *de facto*, a widow. By the time my father retired, the Newark that had sustained him was long dead. Now he was resurrected as a man of leisure without a single interest in the world that had replaced the one that he had known.

My parents' first separation lasted precisely seven days, but the second went on for more than a month. This one was heading into a trimester. Listening on the phone from wintry Boston, first to one side and then the other, I had told myself that the intervals between their getting back together were like inverted labor pains, and thus made a kind of sense: my parents were destroying, not creating. Which evidently took longer than might be imagined.

An eternal moment somehow passes. Lissa's spoon clatters to the patio. In slow motion, I watch Jemma hand hers over and slip an arm around her younger sister's shoulders. My mother keeps walking toward us. She looks older than the last time that I saw her. After my father's first heart attack, I made Michael take her calls. Occasionally I mailed a note, and once, I wrote a letter, but then I ripped it up. In the letter, I tried to explain that I couldn't bear the thought of my father's being alone again. He had been so alone as a child.

In another few seconds, my mother will tell me that the hospital just called to say he had another heart attack. She won't have to say the rest. Of course my father is a goner. Three strikes and you're out, as he would have noted.

I was afraid to go over to the condo. I had planned to stay in Florida until he was released, then return to Boston without even stopping by.

But amazingly, the only hand I lay on my mother when she finally reaches our table does not lash out, does not banish, but pulls her closer toward me.

The Bay Brook Bungalow Colony isn't near the Biscayne Bay or any brook, and it doesn't offer bungalows. It's a land-locked barracks on the sandy highway, a single slab of concrete painted bile-green and bounded by a strip of artificial grass. That my father—"formerly of Short Hills," as Beaver's obituary put it—ended his time here almost keeps me paralyzed in the air-conditioned Buick the next morning. But when Michael turns off the ignition, I tell him I'm okay, and walk toward the little office. The air smells of heat and foulness from the dumpster.

Inside, a small girl in a frilly nightgown is coloring at a table in the corner, her crayons strewn around her on the tiled floor. On a wicker chair nearby, an elderly woman in a faded floral dress is reading a brochure with a picture of a racing horse on the front. The man who must be Marvin Glickman stands behind the counter. Its surface is nearly obscured by a collection of chipped ceramic mermaids. He is talking to an elderly man—the woman's husband. They're trying to figure out how to get by bus to the track at Hialeah.

Everyone stops what they're doing to stare at me when I open the screen door and walk in. I try to smile at the little girl, but she just stares at me.

After a few seconds, Marvin Glickman breaks the silence. "You must be Vic's daughter," he says. "We heard about what happened."

The little girl starts to inch her way to a swinging half-door that lets her get behind the counter. With what appears to be some difficulty, the elderly woman eases herself from the wicker chair and walks over to her husband. They must both be in their eighties, pushing ninety. From her husband's side, the woman says, "You're the lawyer. We met your sister last time. Your father often talked about you. He was very proud."

"Thank you. I'm here to get his things," I say.

"It's such a terrible shame," says her husband.

I start to thank him too, but then Marvin Glickman says, "The way he lived. Alone and all. Your father liked to call me *goniff*, every day, right to my face. But even I felt sorry for him."

"Such a young man," says the woman. "Such a shame."

I should have come much sooner, come the first time, forced my father out of here. On the phone two months ago, I did ask him to live with us in Boston. I should have begged. I should have flown down here and kidnapped him.

"This is only temporary," I say. "He's just here for a short while."

The four of them stare back at me. The overhead fan is whirling, but that's the only sound. The little girl plugs her thumb into her mouth and sidles closer to her father. I feel my face flush when I realize what I said, which tense I'm still using: present. But it's far too soon for past, for permanent. Let the obituary say it.

Marvin Glickman lifts a duplicate key to my father's room from a pegboard and sets it on the counter. "The whole state of Florida is temporary," he says. "But look. I hate to have to tell you this. I really do. Vic owed his last week's rent. And just to set the record straight, I've got a heart. I'm not billing for the days that he was in the hospital. Those days are on me." He lifts his daughter to his hip, eases her thumb from her lips, and folds his fingers over her whole hand. "You'll ruin your teeth," he tells her. And I see that he is just a family man, struggling to survive.

So I open my wallet and pay my father's debt. Michael's outside, waiting in an oasis of shade. Our girls are with my mother. My father's so-called "bungalow" is #23. It's at the far end of the concrete barracks, after twenty-two identical others, and just before the dumpster. The door sticks when I get the key in. Since my father last was here, the heat must have swelled it.

There's no rational reason for this. There's still some money left.

The unmade bed. The sand, and dust, and the forbidden Macanudo's ashes shrouding the surface of the nightstand. The old fedora hanging on a wooden hook. The nomad's opened suitcase, still unpacked. The slatted chair beside the telephone, where he waited for my mother's call. And through the opened bathroom door, the Old Spice and Vitalis on the chipped sink.

But it's the travel-sized tube of the toothpaste my father always swore by that makes me say to Michael, "I can't go in there."

From a distance, Florida looks heavenly. On the flight down from Boston, Michael had to set his watch alarm to signal on the hour, so the girls could rotate at the window seat; this time, heading back up north, they both urged me to take it. From here, I finally can see the Biscayne Bay and the palms along the ocean shoreline, sailboats heading into port, the thin dark ribbon of the Intracoastal winding to its end. Everything is going back to where it ought. The moon is waiting for its cue in a dusky orange sky.

Once, when my sister was Jemma's age, and I was roughly Larissa's, we came down here on spring vacation with my parents. I'm sure we stayed with my maternal grandparents, who, late in life, spent six months of the year in a stucco house on Pine Tree Lane. But it seems to me we met up once with Harry and his family. Could that possibly have been? Might that smoky *seder* have included salt air and several members of my mother's family? I could lean across the aisle and find out. But my mother will wonder why I ask about an ancient celebration of the trek from Egypt, after all these years. I told Michael about Beaver's death, but I haven't told my mother, or that Harry still survives. She probably thinks that only her side will appear at my father's funeral.

Miami devolves into a shapeless green- and blueness, then vanishes entirely. The carts start wheeling down the aisle. Drinks are poured, peanuts proffered. A little later, my mother and the girls get their tiny trays of dinner. Michael accepts the two the steward offers us. I try a bite of the entree, then turn to the darkening window and ease the bit of chicken into the paper napkin I have lifted to my mouth. But Michael sees.

"Honey, please," he says.

"I'm really not hungry."

He takes a bite. "It's not half-bad. You ought to try." He finishes his portion, eats the lettuce salad, sips his coffee. He sets the cup on the tray and drums his fingers on the arm rest. I take his hand and stroke his palm, fiddle with his plain gold wedding band. My mother's wedding band is platinum, set with several diamonds. As girls, my sister and I wore birthstone rings, hers a tiny emerald chip, mine sapphire. Or I wore the red and gold paper rings that my father slid from his cigars and gave me. He never wore a wedding band, or any kind of ring. Later, I realized that many men refuse to. But as a girl, I thought it was because he was an orphan that he couldn't.

"I can't eat that dog food," I tell Michael.

He sighs, and we sit in silence for a while. Then he slides his tray on top of mine, eases from his seat and heads for the steward, who is further up the aisle. They exchange a few words and the steward glances toward the First Class cabin, then turns back and nods. Michael thanks him and returns to me.

"There's a seat open in First Class," he says. "You go and take it. You'll have more room, you'll be more comfortable. The food is better up there."

"I shouldn't leave the girls. We all should be together."

"They'll be fine here. And the movie's starting soon."

He's right, the lights inside the cabin have already dimmed, the screens have just been lowered. Michael could use a break from me, and besides, I've never flown First Class before. The seat is something like a leather sofa. The arm rests are wide enough for thighs. Beside me, a woman about my age is wearing earphones, eyes closed, comfortably transported. Across the aisle, one seat up, a young man in a business suit is working at a laptop, responding to his e-mail. He reads a message, nods, then eagerly types an answer. I watch him for a while: the fingers dancing on the keys, the lines of print filling up the screen importantly. All those words. He pounds them in and then scrolls down, scans the remainder of the message he received—and his fingers freeze. He can't go on. Some new truth has appeared. He hits a key that vanishes his version, and all those words are gone.

The steward brings me dinner: real steak, on real china, with real linen. I take a bite of the pink meat, which goes down fine. Tucked beneath the plate is a gilt-edged card listing various services available in First Class. This morning, when the sun rose and I came in from the balcony, I called in the obituary to *The Suburban Jewish News*, and my father got his first lucky break of late. He just made the deadline for tomorrow's, Tuesday's, paper. In north Jersey, the trucks already are delivering. That's sufficient time, if Harry still subscribes. Jews must bury right away—embalming, like cremation, is forbidden—but the funeral cannot happen until Wednesday, when the coffin gets to Newark Airport. Evidently, a limited number of slots are available for coffins on each flight. Given that this is southern Florida, those slots fill up quickly.

When the steward reappears with coffee and peach melba, I ask him for a cell phone.

"Certainly," he says. "Whatever we can do."

Half of Jemma's friends have cell phones, and the other half have beepers so they can call their parents when they have gotten where they're going, so their parents can call when they'll be late. But Michael and I decided not to go that route. Those parents don't worry any less than we do, despite the high-tech gadgets that they think can stop disaster. But it does seem a kind of miracle to be miles above the spinning earth and hear a human voice still grounded on it. I have dialed northern Jersey information. The young man that I spoke with when I called *The Suburban Jewish News* knew even less than I do about my father's brothers. He had written the obituary, but he didn't have Harry's phone or address, and he didn't know Beaver's actual name. He was so new at the job that his curiosity still ruled him. "I can sense that there's a story there," he told me eagerly.

The computerized information system has failed to find the listing for my surviving uncle. "Harry Tarlow, Union," I tell the human operator who comes on then. She tries all the local towns—Springfield, Livingston, Westfield, Millburn—but Harry isn't listed. I hang up, disappointed but unsurprised: my father wouldn't ever list our number, either.

Yesterday, before I let him go, I whispered in my father's ear that I did remember Harry, clearly.

Of course he's no Messiah, but surely I will know him when I finally see him.

My uncle Harry was in the army, fighting Hitler, when my paternal grandmother died. So my father couldn't live with him. For a long time, growing up, I wondered why he didn't live with Beaver—

The Orphan

why, instead, he had to live out of a cardboard suitcase, grubbing lunches from his teachers, staying with near-strangers here and there, sometimes on the streets or in a dank back room at Newark's Golden Bowling.

Decades later, when I helped my own parents pack up for their exile to Florida, I found a rusted metal box in the basement of the Short Hills house. Inside were fading photographs, documents and letters. I held the pictures to the light, read between the letters' lines, and learned a thing or two. Beaver's oddball appellation came from pulling off the trickiest heists: nickel-'n-dime stuff while my impoverished grandmother was alive, then floating craps games after she died too; eventually, racks of furs off a hijacked truck along the Jersey Turnpike in the middle of a record-breaking blizzard. The second getaway car got stuck in a snow bank. Stranded in the freezing cold, my father's older brother eschewed rabbit, mink and sable to await a tow in floor-length beaver.

The postmark on the letters came from Lewisburg, in Pennsylvania, where he did tony time in the company of men called Sharpy, Shorty, Donut, who dubbed my uncle for the fur that put him there and made my father's childhood a misery, a history that enslaved him even after he, somehow, had trekked through to adulthood. When his brothers returned to Newark, one from the beaches of Normandy and the other from prison, it was only a question of time until their tribal ties frayed and finally vanished like a mirage. What my mother had to do, what she was doomed to fail to do because no human could have, was to make my father forget the howling, needful past, the scourge of abiding loneliness—despite her presence, despite Marlene's and mine.

And so my father worked and he worked and he worked, and it was never enough to make him remember that his life was different now; and over the years, my mother grew further and further away, until she was as distant from him as he had been from his brothers, as an orphaned boy.

In Miami, when I dialed E. J. Teitelbaum & Sons, I signed on for a plain pine box and white shroud with black stripes. None of us ever practiced orthodoxy, but my father said it was the only way to go. "More bang for the buck," he told me in the hospital, as if this, like all eternal truths, was handed down by Moses.

At the funeral home, I am glad to see the rabbi's flowing beard and black *yarmulke* when he shakes our hands and offers his condolences, then produces a small scissors and assists us as we snip gashes in the lapels of our black jackets. My father would say it was crazy to ruin brand-new outfits, but I think secretly he'd wish that we had torn them, as was done in ancient times. And he'd be disappointed by the lack of *payes* curling past the rabbi's temples. But this is well-heeled suburbia, and the only orthodox rabbi that Teitelbaum could get.

My mother, my sister and I are standing at a distance from the opened coffin. We're holding hands, we three surviving women. In a moment, we will view the body before the lid is closed, as per orthodox ritual, and the Hebrew service starts. Years ago, when this mortuary still was located in Newark, we used it for the funerals of my maternal grandparents, so the place seems vaguely familiar: the polished pews; the lamp emitting buttery light beside the coffin; the single, stained glass window. My mother's relatives waiting in the anteroom. The clot of men in black over in the shadowed corner, standing with clasped hands and poker faces.

The rabbi gestures at the opened coffin, and my mother lets go of our hands. She breathes in and takes the first step, then another, toward my father. Marlene and I move into the shadows, so she can be alone with him. I badly want to watch this, but cannot bear to see it, and turn my face away. A moment passes, then another; briefly, I feel almost happy at the length of time she's spending.

Then the cold sun shafts through the stained glass, and I see Harry's face. He's radiant in the corner, among the pale men lingering there. It's him. He has come, as I prayed he would. He is here to be with his brother.

His colleagues move aside, exchanging glances when I step forward. Marlene takes my elbow and leans close to me.

"Those guys washed and stayed with Pop last night," she whispers. "It's what the orthodox do. They sit with him throughout the night, so he won't be alone."

She's right, of course. The man who looked like Harry isn't him at all. He's a total stranger. A mirage.

But this most definitely is not: the absolutely real, uncompromising image of our father wrapped in his white shroud, its silky edges arranged in a sort of fan around his face, the only part of him now visible to humans. I have taken my first step toward the coffin. Then the second. I have nearly reached his side.

He can't stand to see a woman crying. Never could. So I press both hands to my mouth, as if the tears would come from there, and stop one step away from him.

His color still is decent, rather than the awful gray that I expected. His closed eyes, his nose, his slightly open mouth: during the last forty-eight hours, these landmarks have not sunk or shifted. But in his unadorned pine box, my father looks less like a seventy year old man who died two days ago in southern Florida than one who perished on a distant desert near Mt. Sinai. An old, old Jew, an orphan laid to rest, his years of wandering finally at an end.

One last step delivers me to his side.

I'm here.

I reach out and press my damp hand to my father's slightly parted mouth. With the tips of my fingers I can feel his teeth beneath the dry flesh of his lips, the one tooth false but all the others his, enduring. No one goes without a trace, I want to tell him. Bones or ashes, there's no difference, where memory is concerned.

Carnegie Mellon Series in Short Fiction
Editor, Sharon Dilworth

Fortune Telling
David Lynn

A New and Glorious Life
Michelle Herman

The Long and Short of It
Pamela Painter

The Secret Names of Women
Lynne Barrett

The Law of Return
Maxine Rodburg

The Drowning and Other Stories
Edward Delaney

Friends of Carnegie Mellon Press
Series in Short Fiction

Sally Levin, Gerald Costanzo, David Baker, Mort and Rita Seltman, Ellen and Greg Kander, Lou and Amy Weiss, Sabina Deitrick, Vit and Bernie Friedman, Susan Golomb, Megan Gayle, Vera Moore, Eleanor and Bruce Feldman, Walnut Capital Management, Marilyn and Earl Latterman, Mr. &Mrs. Jeffery Cohen, Jack and Andy Weiss, Rich Engel, Jen Bannan, Cathy Lewis, Steve Leper, Jim Daniels, Kristin Kovacic, Pat and Bob Gorzyca, Gretchen A. McBeath, David Lewis, Robert Morison, Susan and Steve Zelicoff